MW00488286

Lex Demirali works, lives, and plays in the New York metropolitan area. Her life includes laughing and loving her friends and family along with the obligatory few moments of sadness. She has extensive experience including selling fixed income products on Wall Street to institutional investors, selling technology, marketing at a law firm, and involvement with philanthropic organizations. While she has an interesting career, her passion is writing to entertain and encourage her readers through their difficult times.

To my sacred family, I am blessed by you. Thank you for
your love and support.

Lex Demirali

THE BAD IS THE GOOD

AUSTIN MACAULEY PUBLISHERS™

LONDON • CAMBRIDGE • NEW YORK • SHARJAH

Copyright © Lex Demirali (2021)

All rights reserved. No part of this publication may be reproduced, distributed, or transmitted in any form or by any means, including photocopying, recording, or other electronic or mechanical methods, without the prior written permission of the publisher, except in the case of brief quotations embodied in critical reviews and certain other non-commercial uses permitted by copyright law. For permission requests, write to the publisher.

Any person who commits any unauthorized act in relation to this publication may be liable to criminal prosecution and civil claims for damages.

This is a work of fiction. Names, characters, businesses, places, events, locales, and incidents are either the products of the author's imagination or used in a fictitious manner. Any resemblance to actual persons, living or dead, or actual events is purely coincidental.

Ordering Information
Quantity sales: Special discounts are available on quantity purchases by corporations, associations, and others. For details, contact the publisher at the address below.

Publisher's Cataloging-in-Publication data
Demirali, Lex
The Bad Is the Good

ISBN 9781647500610 (Paperback)
ISBN 9781647500603 (Hardback)
ISBN 9781647500627 (ePub e-book)

Library of Congress Control Number: 2020917062

www.austinmacauley.com/us

First Published (2021)
Austin Macauley Publishers LLC
40 Wall Street, 33rd Floor, Suite 3302
New York, NY 10005
USA

mail-usa@austinmacauley.com
+1 (646) 5125767

First, thank you to dear Ben, my son, who keeps me grounded and directs me when I am not on target. My wonderful sister and brother, Lee and Jeff, and their spouses have stood beside me through tragedy, trauma, and joy, thank you. My two nephews and their wives, thank you for your support and encouragement to write this book.

I am grateful for all the wonderful and horrendous experiences in my life that became part of this book. While I lived through experiences I didn't want, I learned from the pain. Of course, the fun, joy-filled parts of life provided me with relief and a light heart, which hopefully will bring smiles to all my readers. Thanks to all of you who read this book.

Chapter 1

Victor sat on the toilet.

Nothing new with that picture. But what I heard next was new.

"I'm not happy, Lauren. I want a divorce."

My knees buckled, "What? Divorce? Why? You're kidding, right?"

"No," he snapped, "I'm not kidding. I'm unhappy; miserable, in fact."

Tears welled up as I clung to the sink and stared into the bathroom mirror. Sad blue eyes surrounded by shoulder length bob cut brown hair stared back.

Victor had been moping around for a while, but let's face it; he liked to be sullen. His negative moods gave him a sense of control, particularly over me. For him, there was power in his misery. For me, there was fear.

"Can't I do anything to make this marriage work?" God, I hated myself when I went into the fixer mode. I could hardly fix myself.

"No." What he said next was even more shocking. "It's all your fault, Lauren."

"My fault?" I winced. "What did I do?"

"For one thing, you travel too much. You're not here when I need you."

Travel, it was only a few days a month. And he certainly didn't mind all that my salary bought: nice vacations, expensive clothes, concerts and elegant dinners out.

I was shocked. I tried to be a great wife, sensual lover and best friend; but after all that effort, Victor didn't seem to notice or care. The guy I dated for five years and married seven years ago had been fun-loving and compassionate. But he had changed; he was drowning in his own self-pity, and bourbon.

"Hey, you might want to leave, it stinks in here," he said as he flushed the toilet.

I hurried out of the bathroom choking on the fumes of reality.

"Doesn't our time together matter to you?" I asked as he passed me in our bedroom. "How can you throw this relationship away so easily?"

He smirked, "I'm done."

God, I hated that smirk.

It was only eight in the morning, but Victor headed for his liquor supply. The silence was deafening; I knew he was done talking. This was the beginning of another bender and I was relieved to be going to work.

There wasn't enough tinted moisturizer to cover my blotchy face. "Get it together, Lauren Thorpe," I fumed, now really pissed that Victor thought I was the source of his problems. Heading out the door, I couldn't find my keys – the beginning of a very difficult and long day.

Work was impossible. I skipped returning Hank Tofar's call to follow up on his mortgage request; didn't follow the stock or bond markets and forgot to review the quarterly reports. My only activity was ruminating on Victor. I accomplished nothing and stayed away from my co-workers – behaviors so unlike me.

Victor moved out within a week and stopped calling. Since I purchased the co-op before we were married, I didn't have to find another Manhattan apartment – thankfully. Big Apple apartment hunting can be difficult, and very expensive.

There is nothing to say about mutilated memories of marriage with no hope of reconciliation; but his departure is a relief. I no longer had to deal with his erratic behavior. Coming home to an empty, dark apartment was a significant improvement to a hostile but silent Victor or worse, his rantings of rage.

But, now what?

***

Still mortified at Victor's leaving me, I called my dear friend, Rosemary Haley. The following Tuesday we met for drinks at Harry's, our favorite place in lower Manhattan.

"You mean he asked you for a divorce while he was shitting on the toilet?" Rosemary didn't mince words. I cringed at the crudeness of the situation but talking with her made me feel better.

"I know you made the bulk of the money," she said.

"Yes, and in bed, I dressed up for him, talked dirty, and enthusiastically faked way too many orgasms," I replied.

Yes, I allowed him to be the primary focus of my life – clearly a big mistake. I was to blame for letting myself be used so thoroughly with no emotional or, in fact, any return.

"Well, he was the one swilling down the alcohol," Rosemary said, "not you. It's his fault and loss; quit beating yourself up."

What a true friend. Rosemary was always in my corner.

"You might want to investigate Al-Anon," she suggested. "It's a group for anyone affected by an alcoholic's drinking and behavior. It comes down to abuse; you were abused by Victor. You need to go to Al-Anon so you don't make any more mistakes and jump into a relationship with another alcoholic."

"Great idea, Roe. It is rough living with an alcoholic," I said.

"And for God's sake, relax. Get yourself a massage!"

"Thanks, Roe. Didn't know about Al-Anon and certainly wouldn't have considered a massage. I'll follow up on your suggestions."

"Sorry Lauren, this is not a great time to give you this news, but I've gotten a promotion. I'll be moving to Los Angeles very soon."

"Congratulations, Rosemary," I said pulling her in for a big hug. "You deserve this reward. I'm so happy for you."

My husband leaves; now my best friend too.

How much bad news can one woman take?

Chapter 2

There was a gift waiting for me at the front desk of my building a few nights later. It was a basket of goodies. Tears welled up. How will I ever find another true friend like Rosemary? Her thoughtful words of wisdom and this basket pointed to what I already knew: Rosemary was a true friend and her departure will leave a big hole in my life, especially now.

I lost my appetite just thinking about Roe's departure, but no dinner didn't stop me from unwrapping her basket. She sent vanilla scented body oil, rose milk soap, a scalp and hair oil treatment and a loofah sponge to slough off dead skin from the body. In my case, I knew Rosemary sent me the exfoliator to brush off Victor. Also included was a gift card for five massages at a local spa. That's Rosemary, always following through on her suggestions; that's why the bank needed her in California.

Never having had a massage, nervously I wondered what it would be like. If Rosemary suggested it, I was going to follow through, intimidated or not. It was time to live my life differently.

Clearly, the old way didn't work.

Saturday morning arrived and off I went for my 9:45 massage appointment.

The salon was lovely. Water fell along a wall of rocks into a pool below creating soft, calming sounds. Pale blue walls, gentle lighting and an accommodating, heavy set blonde woman sitting behind a wooden desk made check in easy. The environment was relaxing, but first massage nervousness quickly set in as I waited.

Eventually, I was ushered into a private room for a full body 80-minute massage by Brett. The tall, muscular, handsome masseur politely asked if there were any specific areas that needed attention. I thought about the neglected longing between my legs, but I murmured something about soreness from stress as my husband and I were divorcing.

"I'm sorry for your difficulties; I know how hard divorce is," Brett said sadly. His sympathy felt so real, I wondered if he was divorced.

Brett told me to take all my clothes off and get on the table, face down. He left the room, giving me privacy. I took off my navy sweat pants, bra and a tight, white T-shirt. I've never been big on underpants on the weekends; the commando style made me feel free. With clothes off, I laid on a warm massage table and pulled the sheet over my 5' 9" naked body.

When Brett returned, he dimmed the lights and lowered the music. I could hear him rubbing oil on his hands and arms. He started with a back massage; his warm, oily hands rubbed my back in long leisurely strokes going from the top of the shoulders, over the shoulder blades, down on either

14

side of the spine, past the lower back to the buttock. He stopped just short of the glutes.

I must have been imagining the sensuality of his touch.

"How's the pressure?" he inquired.

Everything was perfect, I told him.

"Do you want the glutes massaged?"

Whoa! The glutes?

"Yes," I drew in a deep breath, "thank you."

I read somewhere that there is a surprising amount of tension and stress located in the derriere, so a buttock massage seemed like a good idea. Besides, it had been too long with no man's hands on my ass. I missed the touch. As Brett kneaded the stress away, I was enjoying my first massage, but was the increasing sexuality in his touch real? Could this twenty something year old masseur be interested in stimulating a 38-year-old soon to be divorced woman?

Brett rubbed my glutes out to the hip muscles. He went from the center and moved to the sides of the rear, slowly massaging my butt and the lower back. He grabbed the meat of the derriere and squeezed the muscles. My vagina pulsated and moistened. The relaxation was now giving way to my heart pumping faster and a growing throbbing between my legs.

Brett came closer to my ear, "Do you want me to massage your upper thighs and between your legs?" he whispered.

My heart skipped a beat – the inner thigh?

I choked out, "Yes."

His hands caressed the inside of my upper thighs. He started by tickling the sensitive skin followed by rubbing warm oil between my legs and then firmly grabbing the

15

inside thigh muscles. The combination caused my breathing to become erratic. It seemed that Brett knew exactly where to touch to stimulate erotic yearnings while still avoiding the slit between my legs. I loved the pleasant sensations but felt self-conscious at the same time.

Brett moved down to my knee and then the calf. After gently circling the knee and almost tickling the inside and underside of the knee, he kneaded the calf muscles. Starting a slow stroke up my leg, Brett continued with a gentle circling motion on each side of the leg as he slowly dug his thumbs into my calf. He massaged his way to my hips. My breath quickened, my cheeks flushed and I swallowed hard as he removed his hands from my leg just before he reached my V.

What is it with this man – even a leg massage is stimulating and erotic. He worked the other leg with equal skill.

Now it was time to roll over. He held up the blanket and asked me to roll over onto my back and move down on the massage table so my head was supported. Then gently laying the sheet over my oiled body; he started working my shoulders and neck.

"There is some stress in your shoulders," he said.

"Oh," was all I could muster.

Every synapse was exploding in my brain. He asked if I wanted my chest massaged. By now I couldn't believe he needed to ask, but I respected his courtesy, answering with a froggy "Yes."

Brett firmly pressed and massaged the chest plate, collarbones, and the rib cage. The muscles gave way to relaxation. Even though he avoided my nipples and circled around the breasts; I felt my nipples harden, shouting for attention.

"Would you like me to rub your stomach?" Brett suggested.

Of course, I submitted. He placed a small towel on my breasts as he carefully folded the sheet to my pubic bone.

The stomach strokes involved a small circular motion starting at the top and center of the rib cage and slowly, very slowly circling down the stomach past the belly button to the pubic bone. I was disappointed when he stopped short of making that stroke much more interesting.

My body was asleep all those years with Victor. Now, in one session, every cell was alive and screaming for his touch.

Brett moved to my hips. Instinctively, they rose off the massage table causing my back to arch. I was horrified that my body was expressing itself and immediately flattened my back on the table. He said nothing and massaged the hip area on the side and the top upper thigh. I was a bowl of pudding. In long strokes, he gently rubbed the inside of my thighs from the top of the leg to the knee. As I fantasized about his touching my clit and putting fingers inside my wet pussy, he lifted his hands off me and said the massage was finished. I wanted to tell him I wasn't.

As I exited the room, I handed Brett a large tip. I tried to wipe the smile from my face as I went to the front desk to take care of the small price for the awakening of my sleeping sexuality.

My plans were to run some errands after the massage, but I had to go home immediately to finish the job I wanted Brett to complete, squirming the whole way home.

Indeed, I was no longer a "massage virgin."

Chapter 3

At work, I became engrossed with my clients; delving into their investment needs, creating new strategies to reduce their liabilities and grow their companies. Working on the private client side of the bank, I advised mid-sized businesses and large family estates on finances, investments, capital structure, tax shelters and large purchases.

"Lauren, you're the top seller this month," Philip Longines, my normally aloof boss said.

"Thank you, Phil."

"Perhaps you should get divorced more often," he said holding up the monthly report.

"You have tripled your production numbers. Keep up the good work." A compliment with a joke about my divorce; that's Phil – passive aggressive.

Not attentive to work issues, my dramatic increase in production caught even Phil's attention. He typically spent his time gambling, looking at racing forms and fantasizing about easy money. If he put as much effort into working as he did gambling, he could have been a successful, wealthy banking executive.

Phil was not a member of the lucky sperm club – he did not come from wealth; but he'd bet and lose thousands of dollars on the horses regularly.

This month's increased production was due to my growing consideration for my clients. I was living differently. I wanted to morph into the best banker I could be. No more halfhearted attempts to sell product to customers. I researched the products, matched them with client's goals and believed my insights could help businesses grow and families increase their wealth. Yes, I was working on changing my thought processes to look at situations realistically, but positively. I was responsible for my life, behaviors and actions. There was freedom and power in owning my life choices, no more blaming, criticizing or resenting Victor.

To service my client, I flew to Miami, Florida to meet with Hank Tofar, a real estate developer. He needed access to $22 million dollars to a purchase a commercial building within eight weeks. While I might have been impatient with Hank for giving me short notice; he called the day Victor announced our divorce. I couldn't respond that day, but today; I was grateful for the challenge.

"Hi Lauren, great to see you," Hank said with flirty enthusiasm.

He guided me to the couch inside his massive office overlooking Biscayne Bay. The aqua water met a light blue sky in the distance, providing a sense of peace and comfort as Hank sat down right next to me.

I noticed his older but still well-defined muscular build, and for the first time, his light blue eyes.

Hank knew that I was going through a divorce and didn't bring it up. It seemed to be everyone's first topic of conversation these days and I was tired of the story. With each telling, I tried to sound less like a victim and more like a successful, grateful, career woman. I was annoyed that I still needed to use Victor's alcoholism to put the blame on him. I'm responsible for my life was my new mantra.

With penetrating blue eyes Hank turned to me said, "I need capital fast, Lauren. Let's use my municipal bonds as collateral for this transaction. This way we can skip some of the paperwork and I can purchase the Ponce de Leon property on time."

Hank was a client on the investment banking side of my firm as well, so it was in everyone's best interest to make sure he could raise the $22 million needed for the down payment to purchase the office building.

"I have a broker waiting at the structure to give us a tour this afternoon. Here are all the financials, closing documents and the leases for the building," Hank said. "Let's go through the paperwork first and then tour the building."

After a thorough review, the paperwork was in order.

I tried contacting the custodial bank to validate that Hank's muni bonds were in his account, but I couldn't get through. I called my boss.

"Phil, can you validate that Hank's bonds are available as collateral for this loan and put a lien on them?"

"Sure," he said, "but you complete the paperwork once you return to the office."

Figures, Phil didn't have time to analyze the racing forms and do his day job.

"No problem," I replied.

After the tour, Hank and I went for a late lunch at La Provencal on Miracle Mile.

"To repeat myself, you look great, Lauren, what are you doing that's different?"

"Thanks, Hank. Victor and I split up. While I didn't want to separate, this divorce is turning into a blessing. I am enjoying my life and the freedom that comes with it."

"Whatever you are doing, it's working. Keep it up."

"Thanks, Hank," I said, feeling uncomfortable about sharing details of my personal life. Secretly, though, I must admit, the male attention was welcomed.

Hank's phone rang, "Sorry, Lauren, I've got to take this call. I shouldn't be long, but I have to finalize some details with a business associate."

He was gone for quite a time. I could hear the tone of his voice both arguing and persuading, but I couldn't make out the exact words in the almost half an hour conversation.

The salads arrived long before Hank appeared and when he returned, he was flushed and distracted.

"What's wrong, Hank?"

"Nothing, I'm just trying to help a friend with a deal and he's not thinking clearly," he replied angrily.

"Do you want to share the details?"

Hank shook his head no.

Phil called me a few minutes later. Sounding stressed, he said the bonds were in place and when I got back to the office, I absolutely needed to complete the paperwork ASAP. I said yes – again.

The timing of Phil's call was perfectly timed with the end of Hank's phone conversation.

Coincidence?

Chapter 4

Back in my office the next day, my assistant called out to me, "Lauren, Hank's on the phone and he says it's urgent."

"Okay, thanks, I'll be right with him."

"Hi Lauren, I'm in town this weekend and was wondering if we could meet Monday after work. I want to talk with you."

"What's wrong, Hank? I gave your documents to the credit department and have your financing lined up for the Ponce de Leon building."

"I'm all set there, but I want to meet to discuss a different topic with you."

"What topic?"

"Your eyes."

"Hank, I'm flattered, of course, but I don't get involved with clients. It's bad for business."

"Lauren, I'm joking. God, you are so serious, take it easy. I want to discuss the particulars of the deal that concern me."

"Sorry, I'm working on fully regaining my sense of humor since Victor's departure. It disappears occasionally. What particulars?"

"Let's discuss the issues Monday. Want to meet at Bouley, 7 PM?" Hank asked.

"Sure, that sounds fine. Are you sure you don't want to discuss what's on your mind now?"

"No, Monday," he said and hung up the phone.

Soon after the call Phil came into my office with a concerned look on his face which typically meant he was losing at the track. Smiles from Phil were rare these days. His obsession with winning fast, easy money from the horses dominated his thoughts, pushing everything, including his job, to the back burner.

"What's wrong Phil?" I asked.

"Rough patch, Lauren."

"I'm sorry to hear that, Phil. At least you get a regular paycheck, have a nice family and the kids are grown and out of the house. Isn't it time to enjoy life?"

"It's not that simple. Money's tight and the wife and I separated two months ago."

"I'm so sorry, Phil. Do you want the name of my divorce attorney?"

"No, we're not getting divorced just yet, I can't afford an attorney. Jenny has been financially dependent on me all these years. Damn, she should be making her own money and not demanding mine. She constantly looks over our accounts and screams about where the money has gone."

Things must be very difficult for Phil to share private details of his life with me.

"Lauren, there might be a mistake in the Tofar account."

"Oh, really, Hank just called me and wants to meet Monday. What is the problem?"

"Hank wants to borrow more money to purchase a building in NYC."

"It's a separate transaction, but that shouldn't be a problem. The bank can provide Hank with another loan. How much money does he need?"

"$16 million."

"What's the problem? Why are you concerned about this transaction? We can put a separate lien on Hank's other assets."

"Lauren, Hank's debt is growing; he's leveraging his real estate holdings."

"Okay, do you want me to talk with Hank and do the paperwork?" I asked.

"Don't call Hank, just do the paperwork for a four-unit condominium building at 3 Sutton Place for $16 million. After you complete the documents, please bring them to me to process."

Weird, I thought. *Phil always has me do the processing. Why does he want to process this transaction?*

"Phil, why would Hank call you and not me?"

"It's complicated, Lauren."

"I've got time to listen."

"Just complete the paperwork and put it on my desk today."

Was Hank buttering me up with the ridiculousness that he wanted to talk to me about my eyes; when what he wanted was additional funding? Was he really that shallow? Did he think I was that gullible?

Chapter 5

Victor was on my mind, but less and less as the days rolled into each other. After a brief denial phase, my extended anger stage was followed by brief periods of bargaining and very mild depression. Acceptance of the loss of Victor came relatively quickly. Before I realized what had happened, I traveled through the five stages of grief.

Perhaps the divorce was in my best interest. Besides, I had more investigative work to do at the massage parlor and I found myself frequently thinking about the handsome 22-year-old blonde. I wanted to go back for another massage and the sooner, the better. I couldn't remember the last time I had been so stimulated and happy with a man's hands on me.

I scheduled a massage with Brett and his magic hands at 10 AM Saturday.

Jumping out of bed Saturday, I showered, shampooed, and shaved my legs, armpits and pubic area into a Mohawk design. I felt like I was going out on a date; even though I couldn't remember the last time I experienced that feeling. Wearing a reasonably tight top and jeans; I was the first appointment of his day. *Perfect,* I thought, *he won't be tired.* In my exuberance, I got to the salon early – so early in fact, that Brett arrived after me. I gave him a big smile when he walked in, but he hardly acknowledged me. Horrified, I wondered if my mind was remembering the last massage correctly.

Perhaps he didn't like me. Maybe he forgot me. Maybe I wasn't pretty enough.

When we were alone in the massage room, Brett asked. "Are there any areas that are sore or in pain that should be worked on?"

I couldn't believe what I was hearing.

Slightly embarrassed, I didn't know what to say.

Brett chimed in, "I wrote down that you got a full body massage last time, is that what you want this time?"

"Yes, thank you," I said in an annoyed tone.

He left the room; I got naked and slipped under the covers. Fuming now, the wait seemed to last forever. Of course, I wanted him to give me the same massage as last time. No, I wanted more than last time.

After stewing about his reaction to me, Brett finally arrived. He started with the luxurious backstroke with his slippery, oiled hands going from my shoulders down to my lower back. He didn't seem to spend as much time on the back as I would have liked, but it was so sensual, my annoyance dissipated quickly as I felt the tingling and gentle waves starting between my legs.

Brett asked, "Do you want your glutes massaged?"

"Yes."

He took his time on the butt and the hips. I felt a release of tension and stifled myself from letting out a moan. He massaged slowly and lovingly with occasionally squeezing my cheeks together and pressing the hips together tightly. I started breathing heavily.

Brett asked, "Do you want your thighs massaged?"

I managed to say that would be nice; trying to sound casual.

He worked his magic on my thighs – he ran his hand across the upper thigh in the crease between my ass and leg and firmly grabbed the inner thigh with his hand. As he massaged leisurely up and down the back of the thigh; my breathing deepened.

He put his hands on each side of the thigh and moved methodically down the leg using circular strokes that caused blood to surge into my groin. He continued slowly down the leg to the calf and gently, slowly stroked the muscles. After he performed his miracles on the other leg; it was time to roll over. Could this be it?

He started massaging my shoulders.

"Do you want your chest massaged?" he asked.

I immediately pulled the sheet from my breasts before I answered. I wasn't thinking; I was lusting. The spontaneous response threw both of us off kilter.

"Oh, sorry, a chest massage would be wonderful," I said trying to compose myself.

He caressed and played with my erect nipples while cupping and fondling my breasts. It was the intimate touch I wanted. He rubbed the muscles on the breastplate and on the ribs while circling around the breasts and nipples. Then he went back to rubbing and pinching the nipples and breasts. This massage was definitely a step above the last visit.

"Do you want your stomach massaged?"

"Yes."

The stomach massage was different from last time. He stood on one side of me, reached to the other side of my stomach and tenderly moved his hands from my far side across the stomach to the near side. It appeared his touch never ended; as one hand came close to him, the other hand started the gentle caress from my far side. He went lower on the stomach ultimately sweeping his hands across my hips and pubic bone. When his stroke passed over my pubic bone, I froze; blood pulsated to my pussy.

I wanted to see if he was hard, but I couldn't get a clear line of vision. What did it matter? He was here to touch me.

His hands softly ran along the crease between the leg and the groin. My body started to quiver. He reached in between my legs and rubbed the inner thighs; occasionally breaking up the inner thigh touch with long strokes down my leg and then back up to move along the crease between the leg and the body and back to the inner thigh. I stopped thinking.

Nothing existed but Brett's touch.

"Do you want me to touch your pubic area?" he whispered in my ear.

What? Did I hear him correctly?

"Yes," I nodded opening my eyes for a moment. He was staring at my pussy. He gently pinched the outside of my lips for quite a while. My head was swooning, my body throbbing.

"Can I go in between your lips?" he asked.

"Please," I begged.

His skilled fingers immediately slipped in between my swollen lips and circled my bulging clitoris. He pulled, rubbed, and prodded, sounding like water lapping as he rubbed inside the labia. I willed myself not to come. I wanted Brett to never stop.

He was in no hurry and I had no sense of time. He rubbed and played with the clitoris for a long time. There was no rush to orgasm, no partner to please and nothing to do except enjoy this moment. And that is exactly what I did. Brett was stroking the clit, with two fingers occasionally delving part way in my vagina. He also rubbed the sensitive inner thigh in between touching my purple button.

My breathing was becoming more erratic; my pussy pulsating and begging for an orgasm. I tried but couldn't hold back any longer. I exploded with my back arching, breathing heavily and legs quivering. The flood of joy didn't stop; I don't know how many times I came. The orgasms were unlike any orgasm I had ever had. The surge of pleasure, the waves of ecstasy kept rising and falling as Brett continually rubbed the magical knob of nerves between my legs. He massaged the clit during the orgasm but gentler after the explosion; which brought me to new heights each time.

He was determined to keep me climbing the crest of ecstasy. I gave into the sensation and rode the surge. The climaxes kept coming; each time taking me to a higher level of pleasure spreading throughout my body and beyond. I wondered if I had ever had an orgasm before Brett. Finally, I breathed deeply and melted into the massage table.

Brett whispered in my ear. Did I hear him correctly? He repeated it.

"Do you want my third arm inside of you?"

Maybe another time.

Chapter 6

Despite repeated attempts on Monday, I couldn't reach the bank to clarify the status of Hank's accounts. Damn, I had a meeting with Hank that night. Phil was nowhere to be found, so I couldn't pump him for extra information or to understand the status of both loans. In addition, I couldn't find where the second loan request was residing in the bank's processing queue.

At the end of the day, I finally got through to the bank to make sure we had Hank's bonds as the guarantee for the first loan and to see if the additional $16 million loan was processed. To my horror, I heard that $22 million dollars was withdrawn from the escrow account.

"What?" Did I hear correctly?

"Who authorized the withdrawal of the $22 million from the escrow account?"

"Oh," the clerk said, "it was Phil."

"Do you have an authorization form?" I asked.

"Yes," she said, "Phil sent it to us, but I haven't seen the document yet. My boss said she received it via fax."

"I suggest you send that form to me immediately. I know nothing about this withdrawal," my voice was rising.

I called Phil's cell phone, but still no answer.

Hank was at the elegant, beige bar, drinking a vodka martini when I walked into Bouley's at 6:55. He looked relaxed, but I was furious – $22 million missing. Really?

"What's going on, Hank? Your $22 million dollars down payment for the Ponce de Leon property is missing and I don't know why you discussed the Sutton Place property with Phil and not me."

"What do you mean $22 million is missing? I do need additional funds for that Manhattan building, but I need to close on the Ponce de Leon building as well."

"What I mean is that the escrow account with $22 million is empty. Phil's not answering his phone and wasn't at work today. The missing money is a big problem."

"I have no idea what is going on, Lauren. You know Phil has a gambling problem and isn't reliable. His financial insights are limited to the racing forms these days and he's not very good at reading those either."

"Then why did you talk to him about the second loan and not me? I'm talking with you first as a courtesy because you are an important client of the bank. This is theft. I've got to report this robbery to our executives tonight."

"I'm sure there's some rational explanation, Lauren. Phil couldn't have taken the money."

"I know Phil has been under financial pressure lately," I said, "but he is not stupid, and I don't think he is desperate enough to rob his employer. I'm asking you again: what is going on?"

"Lauren, that's partly why I called you here to meet me. Phil is in a financial mess. He owes bookies $1.45 million;

his wife is furious; they are separated, and he believes he will be fired soon."

"That's bad news, but why are you involved in Phil's mess?"

"We're related through marriage. Phil's wife is my ex-wife's sister."

"Okay, you are related, but why is $22 million missing?"

"I don't know about the missing money, but Phil also fears for his life. He thinks the bookies will kill him. Phil is the one who brought me the NYC property opportunity, that's why you weren't included. I told him if he could get the loan for the NYC property, I would pay him a finder's fee and part of the cash flow of the deal."

"Hank, why be so secretive about the second loan? You are creditworthy, there's no reason to sneak around. I'm your account manager, why not come to me for the loan? I completed the paperwork, but I don't know where the documents are in the process for the second loan. I gave Phil the docs because he demanded that he process them. Now I can't find them in the system."

"There are some draconian rules in place to purchase the Manhattan building. The oppressive guidelines are: we must close within two weeks and the entire payment must be in cash. It is only a four-flat building, but the homes are three-bedrooms with three baths and are glorious units. It is in lovely Sutton Place. You know how hard condominiums are to find in Manhattan, most residential buildings are those ridiculous co-op structures. The problem is I must come up with $16 million immediately. The monthly fees from the apartments are more than double the cost to maintain the building. This is a lucrative deal. You have to recognize that, Lauren."

"Hank, you're not thinking straight. There could be something drastically wrong with the building or the structure of the deal. You know someone is usually hiding something when a real estate purchase is a rush job."

"I know, Lauren, but I checked the building myself and went through all the paperwork. Everything is in order. I want to help Phil. I'm bringing him in on this deal, so he can pay back his loan. The owners of the building are connected to the people that Phil owes money. They'll kill him if he doesn't pay his loan. I'm meeting with you to see how we can help Phil."

"The owners are bookies? Why are you risking your neck by working with the mob? If they don't like an aspect of the deal, they don't go to court to settle the dispute, they kill you."

"I know, I've checked, and double checked everything. I love this building and want to live there. I don't get involved emotionally with my real estate purchases, but I'm obsessed with this building. So, I'm helping Phil; he gets the finder's fee, 5% of the $16 million. That's $800,000, which is more than half the money he owes them. He'll have to get on a payment plan for the other $650,000 he owes. He'll get some monthly cash from this deal and start making regular payments. At least, he'll be able to survive in the near term."

"You are insane, Hank. This deal is fraught with problems, not to mention the real issue is Phil's compulsive gambling, which hasn't been addressed. He'll gamble until he loses everything and is killed. I don't think he can stop even though he racks up mountains of debt. He needs help for his addiction, which is beyond the expertise of either one of us."

"I have to help, Lauren. My ex is making my life miserable if I don't provide Phil with some income."

"Hank, do you know where the missing $22 million is?"

"No."

"I don't know where the second loan request is located. This is a nightmare, are you sure you don't know where the missing $22 million is?" I asked.

"I don't know. I've raised cash by closing on a residential co-op in the city – if I don't get the $16 million from your bank – but would prefer not to use those funds. Damn, I should not have put Phil in charge of the financing, he's inept. I want to close on Ponce de Leon property as scheduled, but now with the funds missing, that deal may go south."

"Hank, I have to go to our executives. This is a big problem. This is illegal activity, theft and fraud. Plus, you know Phil can't handle these transactions. It is hard for him to complete anything. He asked me to complete the paperwork, but said he'd process the paperwork. I haven't seen any progress on the second loan."

"I talked with Phil today. He's working on it."

"No, he's not. Phil wasn't in work today. Where did he say he was? What time did you talk?"

"I don't know, Lauren. He was acting squirrely."

"Squirrely how?"

"He sounded like he was in the streets, with horns blowing and he wasn't interested in discussing the deal I created for him or my loan progress. Weird right? He was in a hurry to get me off the phone. He can't be involved with the missing $22 MM, Lauren."

Cringing, I asked, "Could someone at the custodial bank take those funds? It doesn't seem possible. It has to be Phil."

"I don't think so, Lauren."

"Given that you were helping Phil and didn't share those important details with anyone at the bank, you put my employer in a precarious position. Plus, as I see it now, Phil or someone at the custodian bank stole $22 million. Where else could that money be?"

"You are over reacting. I'm sure there's a reasonable explanation for the missing money. I really want the Sutton Place condo building. The owners wanted cash and a limited paper trail. That's why the price was attractive. If the market doesn't tank, I can sell this property in two years for double what I paid, but I'll probably live there."

"Compelling reasons for the purchase Hank, but you are forgetting about a $22 MM robbery. Plus, your partners are dangerous."

"I've worked with worse."

"Not the kind that kill if they are annoyed at you. Waiter, a red wine, and hurry."

Chapter 7

Tuesday entailed going through all the documents line by line providing justification for the transactions and repeatedly talking with the bank's executives and lawyers about the missing $22 million. My life, recently on the upswing was headed fast into a downward vortex.

Phil was nowhere to be found; I had to answer the attorney's ugly questions and there were plenty. He had not processed the authorization document for the second loan, but a form approving the release of the $22 MM with my signature on it surfaced. It looked like my signature, not a forgery. Phil had somehow changed the application I completed to a funds release document.

Desperate, I called Hank for back up, but Hank wasn't returning my calls.

A sinking feeling in my stomach tied it in knots.

Despairing, I suffered through sweltering heat in the subway to get to Hank's Manhattan apartment: only to find it empty – of everything: furniture, rugs, lamps, and TVs. The doorman confirmed Hank moved with no forwarding address. Tears uncontrollably poured out of my eyes and didn't stop. Staring through the fog I looked up when the house was sold on my cell – only two days ago. Hank had been a busy man. I saw him last night and didn't remember him discussing the sale of his private Manhattan residence.

Could Hank really be involved with the robbery at the bank? And pick up a nice building from shady characters in the process? Why did Hank disappear? I trusted him; clearly, I misplaced my trust. A*gain.*

After Phil's wife threw him out, he rented a small studio in Kips Bay. It was unlikely he was there since Hank was in the wind, but I had to check. Phil wasn't there; but at least his things were still in place.

Following the money transfers was my only hope for exoneration. I certainly didn't have the funds – that would prove my innocence; I prayed.

I talked repeatedly with company attorneys and told them what I knew. The question that kept on coming up was why my signature was on the release authorization form. My claims that Phil was responsible fell on deaf ears.

The other problem: the woman at the custodian bank who said Phil authorized the release of funds, had the documentation with my signature. Since the release document had my signature on it, she said I authorized the release. Yikes. She changed her story.

There was an all-points bulletin put out on both men. The lien on the municipal bonds could be executed to cover the $22 million, but my bank was responsible for the escrow account until the assets were transferred.

My bank placed me on leave at the end of day – for an indefinite period; probably forever.

***

Two days later Phil was spotted in Las Vegas; not a smart place for a compulsive gambler. Authorities brought Phil back to New York for what I hoped was the end of the nightmare. Phil knew the authorizing document had my signature on it. He was in the clear and denied knowing anything.

"What," Phil said, "the money is missing from Hank's account? How did that happen?"

I was stunned at such blatant lies.

"Why were you in Las Vegas, Phil?" I asked.

"I wanted to take a few days off, so I went to Las Vegas."

"Did you pay off your bookies with the money that Hank gave you for finding him the four-unit apartment building at Sutton Place? Or did you steal the $22 million and have a $22 million gambling spree?"

"What are you talking about, Lauren?" His fake innocence was sickening.

Blood raging through my body, stomach churning; I wanted to stab Phil in the heart – repeatedly. I couldn't believe his transparent lies.

"Where's Hank?" I asked.

"I don't know, but last we talked, he was headed to Florida."

"Why?"

"I don't know. Hank and I aren't that close."

"You are according to the wives – they are sisters. Why are you lying?"

"Lauren, you are the one who signed the release form; is that why you are hostile?"

"Phil, this is a very serious charge that includes jail time. We will both lose not only our jobs, but our careers and lives as we know them. Why did you frame me?"

"Lauren, I didn't frame you."

"Yes, you did, but no worries; they'll follow the money which will lead to you or you and Hank. I will be exonerated."

"Don't be too sure, Lauren."

"Phil, what did you do? How could you drag me down into your schemes? Why?"

"Lauren, I have responsibilities. I had nothing to do with whatever arrangement you think I planned."

"You are an awful human being, Phil. You know I'm suspended from my job until this investigation is over. And now my career in this industry doesn't look viable in the long run. I'm looking at jail time, Phil. Can you live with yourself if I go to jail?"

"I'm telling you for the last time, Lauren; I didn't do anything."

"You are lying, Phil." The conversation was circular and useless. I went home praying that the wire transfers would proclaim my innocence.

Chapter 8

My life was too involved with addicts. This recurring theme in my life caused me to remember Rosemary's suggestion to go to an Al-Anon meeting. Perhaps I should have gone to a meeting earlier, but unfortunately, this was a lesson that had to ruin my life *again* before I heeded the advice.

Wednesday night I walked into my first Al-Anon meeting – very depressed. The yoga pants stuck to my sweaty body from racing to catch the subway; plus, I hadn't showered that day and most likely, the day before. I was losing track of my life. Clearly, I wasn't there to make a good impression. I hoped I didn't know anyone. All Angels Church on West 80th Street seemed to be a safe bet; it was on the west side of the city; my world was on the east side and downtown.

Twenty or so chairs were in a circle in one of the church's basement rooms. The people were friendly and happy, which only aggravated me. I was jobless, under suspicion for robbery, depressed and not showered – an ugly combination. Men and women alike were greeting each other with hugs as they took their seats. A few members tried to hug me. I withdrew. I was in no mood to be hugged. But I must admit, the gesture was welcoming.

Guidelines of behavior were read out loud as well as the 12 steps of Al-Anon. The format of the meeting was to have a participant read a daily meditation from the book *Courage to Change* and discuss how the disease of alcoholism affected their life as it related to the reading.

After the first participant finished, another person chimed in discussing their own experiences and how they identified with the reading. No one interrupted or made suggestions on how to improve a situation. It created a safe place to share; no one was making recommendations or worse, highlighting how a situation was mishandled. I listened, too embarrassed to talk about my circumstances.

About halfway through the meeting, I noticed a quiet, young woman sitting a few chairs from me. She had long blonde hair, but no sparkle in her deep brown eyes. *Had she suffered as much as I had?*

The stories about drunken husbands or wives cheating, beating, stealing and lying were heart wrenching. They reminded me of life with Victor. Even Phil's gambling, lying, stealing and cheating would fit in here. I wondered what the blonde's story was. I knew she had one, why else would she be here?

I sensed no one came to a 12-step meeting on the eagle's wings of victory. I was there only because life had me on my knees; I was desperate. I needed help to live a better life. Judging from the stories, it seemed I was in the right place. Some of the participants appeared genuinely happy and able to cope and enjoy their life, despite their history.

After the meeting, most stayed to talk, hug and drink coffee. As I headed for the door, I saw the blonde getting ready to leave as well.

"Is this your first meeting?" I whispered.

"Yes, is it that obvious?"

"I'm no expert; it's my first meeting too," I answered. "But my head is spinning from the stories I heard tonight."

"I thought about sharing, but I felt too awkward; I was relieved just to listen tonight."

"Yeah, I'm not ready to share my deep dark secrets to the group, either. You want to grab a cup of coffee?" I asked.

The pretty blonde girl's eyes lit up as she stuck out her hand. "Great idea. My name is Greta."

"Hi Greta, I'm Lauren."

We walked to City Diner on Broadway in the 80s. It was an art deco style diner with warm lighting, comfortable booths and an attentive staff. I ordered a Greek salad and Greta ordered a grilled Reuben sandwich with fries.

"What brought you to this Al-Anon meeting?" Greta asked.

"I came to the west side because I live on the east side. I didn't want to run into anyone I know."

"That's not what I was really asking. I meant what's going on in your life? Something has to be awful for you to come to an Al-Anon meeting."

"You're right, Greta. I don't know why I tried to dodge your question, sorry. The short version is my alcoholic husband recently asked for a divorce, so we're separated and working to finish our divorce agreement quickly. Then, as luck would have it, my boss is a compulsive gambler and set me up to take the fall for his $22 million robbery of our employer. At least it appears that it was my boss; but I really can't be sure. Things are unclear right now. Banks don't take kindly to employees with sticky fingers. Obviously, I'm currently not working, but hoping to be exonerated soon. I don't want to end up behind bars."

"$22 Million? That's more than sticky fingers! That's a damn good story, Lauren. I don't know if I can top that."

"It's not a competition, Gretz. Can I call you that?" She nodded yes. "I don't want to be the winner for the most debilitating story. What's going on in your life?"

"Alcoholic ex-husband, to start – just like you. An overbearing and controlling mother married to my alcoholic father, who passed away three years ago. I'm living with my mother who thinks she knows what is best for me. Her vision for me and what I want to do are worlds apart, let's just leave it at that."

"I'm sorry, Gretz. Life is a relentless teacher. Even when I don't want to learn the lesson; it seems the universe keeps giving me the same story with different characters until I learn how to deal with an addict's challenges gracefully. Hopefully, I'll change my thinking by going to these meetings. I don't want to deal with more craziness from addicts, or rather, I want to learn how to handle the craziness without the behavior crushing my soul."

"In some way though, Greta, I think we're all addicts. I'm addicted to always being right and controlling things."

"I hear you, Lauren, and change is what I'm gonna do as well. I'm opening a women's help center. Women are underserved in areas of physical and sexual abuse, violence and mental manipulation. Why should men be able to treat women so poorly, or worse, beat and/or rape them? Women need to have a safe place to go to be healed. We need options."

"Wow, you've got a plan. That's impressive; it's more than I have. Love that idea! Interestingly, enough, since I've been laid off from the bank, I started thinking about opening a financing agency that specializes and caters to women. I need to determine where I'll get the money to lend, but banks and financing organizations deny women's loan requests more than men's loan requests. We need a financing group that caters to our needs."

But how?

Chapter 9

Good news finally broke. Hank contacted me. He was back in NYC from Florida. He bought Sutton Place with the money he received from selling his NYC home, which is why his place was empty. The bad news – Phil used the loan request I completed for the four-unit Sutton Place to forge the documents and withdraw $22 million.

Co-op's in Hank's former Manhattan building were in big demand and he received 30% more than the asking price the first day his co-op was on the market. Because of the strong demand, Hank insisted that they close quickly, and the buyers agreed. I guess Hank really did like the four-unit condo building in Sutton Place.

At least, I understood why his unit was suddenly empty, but wondered why he didn't tell me the news at dinner. We were not sharing details of our personal life, but not to let me know that he was selling his own home to fund the purchase of the Sutton Place property seemed odd. Hank was a private man, but this information would have saved me some stress even though I was still on the hot seat.

Tracing the money through wire transfers was proving more difficult than the bank originally anticipated. The money was sent to Cayman Islands and then divided between Switzerland and back and forth to the Bahamas and Bermuda and then back to the Caymans. Who knew Phil was so clever? I suspected he had help – was it from his loan sharks?

***

Hank called me; he was furious. He helped Phil and this was how Phil showed his appreciation. Now Hank is mad? Why not Monday night when I first told him about the missing money?

"Lauren, we have to meet," Hank said.

"Why? I'm out of a job, a career and a life because of you and Phil."

"Lauren, I'm sorry. I had no idea Phil was going to steal that money."

"Why don't you tell the bank? They think I'm richer by $22 million."

"I did, but *WE* have to go to Las Vegas to trace Phil's path while he was there."

"Have a nice trip, Hank. I don't trust you. I'm not going with you."

"Lauren, I understand. I made mistakes: I trusted Phil and I didn't share my plans with you. I'm so sorry. I did reference that I sold a co-op, which was my Manhattan home, Monday night, but you weren't listening. Please know that I want to make this right. I'll use my financial services contacts to get you another job."

"Hank, that won't work. I will lose all my licenses to work in this business. A suspected bank robber isn't on top of the hiring list for banks. I can't work in this business recommending investments without the proper certifications. I have to change careers."

"I feel terrible, believe me. I need you to help me because you worked at the bank. It lends more creditability to my inquiries and you have a better understanding of the money flow within the bank than I do. I can't get anyone else from the bank to help me, that's for sure. I'll pay for everything, Lauren. You'll have your own suite; I'll fly you first class and give you $5,000 of spending money to come to Las Vegas."

"No."

"I don't think you understand the gravity of this situation. You are going to jail for theft if we don't find evidence that Phil stole this money. I also look bad because it was my transactions that created the opportunity for the theft and I was bringing Phil into the Sutton Place deal, which he didn't report to the bank. The evidence is in Las Vegas. I know a few bookies who will help me get to the bottom of this problem," Hank pleaded.

"Again Hank, you lied and deceived me. You and Phil put me in this position."

"I know, Lauren, I owe you. But if you don't come with me, I won't be able to get the evidence required to acquit you and reinstate my reputation. I thought Phil could process the loan quickly since he was going to benefit from the transaction. He didn't; I had to sell my Manhattan place to get the Sutton Place deal done. Believe me, I didn't want to sell my own home, damn him. I need your skill set. The bookies aren't going to rat on one of their favorite customers unless I have your knowledge with me. I need you to go with me to Las Vegas, Lauren, otherwise you could end up in jail."

"Damn it, Hank, I'll go, but I'm not happy about this arrangement. I'm agreeing because I don't want to go to jail."

"I understand," was all he said.

***

With few glimpses of pleasurable moments in my life, it was fun to fly first class. The stewardesses waited on me with hot towels, a blanket and a glass of cheap white wine. I gratefully drank the wine at 10 AM. The affect was drowsiness. I closed my eyes and dreamed about a life with no jail time.

Hank was at the airport to pick me up. He was full of information. He met with a well-known bookie in Las Vegas. Everyone knew Phil was in town to settle his debts and bet big. That was good news; perhaps this was an effective use of my time.

"Lauren, did you know Las Vegas means *the meadows* in Spanish? There were desert springs which attracted Indians and travelers to Vegas. Young men came here to build the Hoover Dam during the depression, which gave sin city its start in adult entertainment."

"I thought the mob brought adult entertainment to Vegas," I said.

"No, but they built the first hotels. The first one was The Flamingo, which Bugsy Siegel constructed. He named the hotel because his girlfriend had flamingo legs – long and thin."

"Nice love story, Hank," I said sarcastically. "Especially considering Bugsy was killed leaving his girlfriend's home."

"You are correct, but while the mob is in town, they don't run the city the way they used to. Once Howard Hughes invested in Las Vegas, he changed the environment from mafia to corporate, the whole landscape changed."

"So, we are not talking with the mafia? How disappointing," I said mockingly.

"Well, not exactly. The gangs, the Crips, Bloods and Surenos have more influence than people like to admit. But we'll be talking with a member of the Bonanno family, Vinny Green. Phil was old school when it came to borrowing money."

Hank's tone had an edge to it. Was Vinny Green dangerous?

When we arrived at the Bellagio, Hank was trying to lighten the mood, but I could tell he was concerned about our meetings.

I had been to Las Vegas three years ago for a conference. I had a feeling this trip was going to be significantly different than my first trip. Last time, I got up early, worked out, spent all day at lectures and team building exercises, only to eat a late dinner and go to bed. Many of the other attendees spent the night drinking, gambling and finding love where they could. That was not my style; at least back then it wasn't my style.

Hank's suite was close to mine, which caused me some concern, but the looming meetings and jail time trumped any bravado from him. Thankfully, Hank made no subtle sexual suggestions; at least not yet.

**

I dropped off my suitcase and two hours later, Hank and I were sitting in Vinny's elaborately decorated office. I could feel my heart pounding. A heavyset man sat behind an ornate pecan desk with sculptured lion heads springing out of the corners and paws at the base of the desk. I felt that the lions wanted to pounce on me. The floor was green marble with large tufted brown leather sofas and large green, cream and brown oriental rugs that highlighted the different sections of his massive office.

Hank and I sank into the largest sofa after Vinny directed us to the couch. Vinny moved to the couch across from us. His eyes pierced through me. Hank assured him that I was a victim of Phil's theft and use to work for the bank. He assured Vinny that I wasn't law enforcement. Vinny didn't care about our story. He wanted Phil to continue gambling and was not forthcoming with information about Phil or the money he spent.

Hank shot up from the couch and menacingly lurched toward Vinny, "I lent you $50 million so you could purchase this hotel. It's time you helped me. If you don't, I'll tell the Cohen family about your execution of their captain so that you could purchase this hotel."

I flinched to think someone was murdered so Vinny could own this establishment.

Hank continued the assault: "Phil's done gambling, he has no more money and he is going to jail and won't be released for years," Hank snarled. "The bank was robbed by one of their own; they will prosecute with every lawyer they have. Phil's going away – until he dies or is murdered in jail."

"Lauren," Hank asked, "how long can the bank put Phil away if he is convicted?"

"Bank robbery is a federal crime covered under Title 18, section 2113 of the US Code. The bank will try to convict Phil for several crimes: conspiracy to rob, entering the bank with intent to commit a felony and fraud. The bank will try to get consecutive rather than concurrent sentences so, he serves the maximum time in prison for each penalty separately rather than serving the same time due for each penalty. Sentences for convicted bank robbers typically run in the 20-year range, but Phil could be in prison for 55 years if his sentences are consecutive. Phil is 52; it is unlikely he'll be released from prison and still be able to work and gamble if convicted."

"Thank you," Hank said, "I knew you'd know the details."

Sneering, he turned to Vinny. "Do you think Phil is going to remain a good customer? You'll be lucky if they don't trace the money to your operation. Tell me where he went and how much money he dropped at each place. I know everyone talks in this town."

"I can handle the feds," Vinny barked. "But Phil has outlasted his usefulness. Get off me, Hank. As far as I know, here's what Phil did in Vegas."

Chapter 10

Sipping red wine at the Andiamo Italian Steakhouse was the first time in weeks that I considered I might not be going to jail. If we can prove where Phil spent the money, perhaps there is hope.

The red wine soothed and calmed my body. I was not going back to the bank, the release document had my signature on it, but losing my job looked like a slap on the wrist compared to jail time.

"We have two more meetings tomorrow before we can establish Phil's spending spree was because of the $22 million he stole from the bank. My attorney said you will be exonerated if we trace the bank's money to Phil. It is time to enjoy today's victory. Even though this is a chain restaurant, it's one of my favorite eateries in this town," Hank said.

"You know a lot about this town: the history, all the players, spots to eat, where to stay and who to meet. How did this happen?"

"I spent a few years here developing major real estate projects. I loved building and financing casinos, hotels, convention halls and one huge home for an entertainer."

"Why did you leave?"

"My wife didn't like Vegas and I had an opportunity to renovate office buildings in Manhattan. I wanted to come home, so we headed east. Of course, that didn't make my ex content; she'll never be happy, but I was gratified by the work."

Wanting to avoid any spouse conversation, I asked, "What's next on our agenda for tomorrow?"

"We have two meetings, thanks to Vinny. The first meeting is with a well-known bookie, Fat Tony. If we learn what we need to know, then we'll meet with the floor manager where Phil gambled. It'll be the casino that Tony recommended to Phil and most likely, where Phil spent the bank's cash."

"Let me guess, Tony is heavy," I said.

"No, he's short and thin. Smokes cigarettes non-stop. Lauren, I'm sorry about this mess Phil put you in. I had no idea he was so evil."

"He's an addict, Hank. He'll do anything to continue to gamble. I'm just starting to understand the power of addictions," I said.

"Okay, I hear you. It's the last time I listen to my ex. She thought she could help her sister by solving Phil's debt situation, but in truth, the finances are only a symptom. Phil must stop gambling. I can't imagine why he stole $22 million to come to this town; his immediate financial problems were partly resolved. He's crazy."

Shifting in his chair, Hank blurted out, "Lauren, I want to talk about you, not Phil."

"No, Hank. We're here to resolve this problem, Phil has to be our focus."

"I'm attracted to you, Lauren," he continued, ignoring my comment. "I want to know you better than just a working relationship. You are one smart, beautiful lady. I love your attitude, inquisitive blue eyes and a smile that makes the sun shine and my heart pound. I enjoy your company. In fact, I always look forward to seeing you – no matter how difficult the situation."

"Thank you, Hank, I'm flattered, but I'm not interested. Your side deal provided a way for Phil to deceive me. In addition, you were not forthcoming with information about the Sutton Place residence and selling of your Manhattan co-op. I was lost for the first few days after the robbery. Why didn't you return my calls?"

"Phil pulled a fast one. I had no idea he was planning to steal that money. I was busy in Florida and didn't listen to my messages. I contacted you as soon as I heard. I did mention Monday at Bouley's that I had a backup plan if the bank couldn't provide the funds, but I was vague about the details, sorry. I should have made it clear that I was selling my home, but I was hoping the bank would provide the loan. I thought it best to be quiet and let Phil determine how to handle the situation with the bank and you. I didn't foresee him stealing those funds. Believe me, I regret this whole situation more than you'll ever know."

"Let's resolve this issue, Hank. I appreciate your help; but I don't mix pleasure and business."

"You aren't at the bank, Lauren. You're not mixing your lives. I'm hoping we are in a transition phase from working together to sharing our personal lives. I'll help get you another job and follow you to your next job as a client;

if that helps you. No pressure, no need to rush anything. You call the shots. I just want to be with you."

"Hank, thank you, but I'm not interested."

"Really, you're not interested? That's not what I'm feeling when I get next to you."

"Ok, yes, there is heat between us, but I'm not getting involved. My relationship with you got me here."

"No, it didn't. My deal was with Phil. He stole the money and set you up, not me."

"Okay, good point, but I'm not interested. I can't work in the financial services industry; I have to explore other career paths."

"That won't happen, we are closer to putting Phil away with every meeting and you will be vindicated. "

***

Getting in the shower the next morning was difficult with two glasses of red wine in me from the night before, but the hot water brought me back to life.

I met Hank in the lobby. "Good morning sunshine. Did you sleep well?"

God, he was cheery in the morning. "Yes, thanks, how about you?"

"I went to bed thinking about you. I had a nice time last night and missed you when we went to our separate rooms. I can't stop thinking about you."

"Hank, can we stay on the Phil topic today?"

"Sure, let's get a cab to see Fat Tony."

Thirty minutes later, out in the Nevada desert we came to a single floor adobe building with only two windows covered with bars located in the front of the building. Standing at a metal back door with several locks above the knob, Hank made a call.

"Yeah, we're outside the back door. No, it's a woman from the bank; she's the one Phil set up to take the fall for his robbery. No, she's not law enforcement; she's going to jail if we can't follow the money trail."

My eyes widen, sweat appeared on my upper lip under the beating sun and faced with reality. I glanced at Hank. As he stepped out of sight of the camera, he was waving his hand in the air in a "don't worry" signal.

In a dark room reeking of beer and cigarettes, Hank threaded his way through stacked chairs and tables to an office on the other side of the room. "Hi Tony, thanks for seeing us."

"What information do you want, Hank? I'm busy."

"Nice to see you too, Tony," Hank replied flatly.

This meeting was not off to a great start.

"We need to determine where Phil spent the $22 million, he stole from the bank."

"Look Hank, I don't want any trouble with you or the Feds, but Phil paid me the $1.45 million loan he owed and spent $16.4 million on a gambling spree that boosted my books for the week."

"So, Phil spent $17.85 million through you?"

"Yes."

"Which casino did he patronize?"

"The Palazzo."

"How big a cut did you get by sending him to the Palazzo?"

"17%."

"You earned $3,034,500 by sending Phil to a specific casino?" I chimed in incredulously.

"Yes."

"Thank you, Tony. I'm glad you had a good week, but Phil's going away for quite a long time," Hank said.

Hank had the cab wait for us. As we got in the car, Hank was visibly happy with the outcome of the meeting.

"What was the good news in that meeting?" I asked.

"The Palazzo keeps records of Phil's gambling because they had to pay commissions to Tony. That's great for us; we have proof Phil spent over $16 million at the casino. There's only one place where Phil got those funds. Phil had to use the bank's funds to do this type of gambling. The question is: where is the other $4,150,000?"

Hank had the cab driver take us to the Palazzo. The casino was located on Las Vegas Blvd with its own beautiful archway entrance. The valet opened the door for us. Hank jumped out and charged into the casino. He headed to the back of the casino; I had trouble keeping up. I couldn't detect the office door until Hank opened it by pushing the sconce on the wall. The casino was filled with marble, large crown moldings, beautiful columns, lush furniture and lights everywhere. The door to the office had molding that matched the walls and was not visible to the untrained eye.

Hank barged into a library style office. The floor manager jumped up from his desk and was reaching for his revolver when he recognized Hank.

"What the hell are you doing here, Hank? I haven't seen you for years."

"Hello John. It's been six years, at least. How's business?"

"Can't complain. We have good weeks and slow days. Why are you storming into my office?"

"It's Philip Longines. He was here last week and spent."

"I know, Hank," interrupted John, "he spent over $16 million with us. Quite a spree, I'd say."

"Thanks for the update, John. He stole the money from the bank where he worked and framed this woman, Lauren, for the robbery."

"Uh-oh, what do you need from me?"

"I need the documents outlining the $16.4 million he spent here at your beautiful casino."

"No problem, Hank."

"It's great to have you as a friend, John, thanks."

"I can provide you with video as well. Can you stay for a drink?"

"Sure. Lauren, you up for a drink?"

"Yes, thanks."

"Lauren is the one who has the most to lose here, John. Phil framed her to take the fall for his robbery. Phil deceived her and somehow got her signature on a funds release form. It was my transaction that gave Phil the opportunity to steal the money."

"Sorry to hear the news, Lauren," John said. "Phil stole money from MGM last year, they have it on tape, but they didn't prosecute because they didn't want the publicity. He took about fifty grand, but I'm not sure of the exact amount."

"Really? Phil's pilfering from everyone, I wish I had the info last year." I sighed.

"If I knew, I would not have offered Phil a partnership in my real estate deal, either. Sorry, Lauren," Hank said.

"You know Hank, I think Phil would have used me to rob the bank whether it was your account or someone else's money. I was on his radar as the fall guy."

"Sounds like we'll need a bottle of chilled vodka, lemons, a few capfuls of vermouth and three chilled martini glasses." John told his assistant.

Sipping the beginning of my second martini, I realized I hadn't eaten all day. Hank read my mind and said, "John, we're going to Aquaknox for dinner, you want to join us?"

"No, I'm going home to my sweetie tonight. Thanks for the offer."

Hank grabbed my arms and gently pulled me off the couch. He slipped his hand around my waist to help me balance.

"John, I'm in your debt, thank you for the files. With any luck we'll be back next year to celebrate this day."

"You hungry, Lauren?" Hank asked.

"Yes, thank you."

"You up for caviar? Aquaknox is a short walk from here. Are you okay to walk? I know martinis are rocket fuel."

"I can walk Hank, thanks," I said as I unsteadily moved one foot in front of the other.

Hank offered a cocktail as we sat down to dinner, but I had the good sense to say, "No thank you."

Dinner was delicious; warm foie gras and chilled caviar. My low caviar consumption was due to the exorbitant price of those salty eggs. But, with martinis in me, I didn't care about cost, it was time to celebrate. Normally, I would not stick a man with an expensive tab, but Hank ordered several ounces for his dinner and I wanted to celebrate as well.

He put his hand on my thigh and stared lovingly into my eyes, "Lauren, I think we have enough evidence to put Phil away. The lawyers can prove that Phil withdrew the funds from the bank, flew directly to Vegas and went on a one serious gambling bender. You are going to be okay."

"Thank you, Hank. I would not been able to get this evidence without you. You did all the work. I owe you Hank, thank you."

"That's great to hear; I'm glad you appreciate my efforts," he said as he snuggled closer to me.

"Lauren, I want you; want to know more about you." His warm, moist breath was hitting my neck, triggering a desire for Hank to kiss and lick me.

"Thank you, Hank." I closed my eyes and thought about putting my arms around him, kissing him, but I was embarrassed.

Hank broke the silence that was filled with sexual thoughts, "Would you like a night cap at the hotel?"

"No, thanks." I was sure I didn't want to get naked with Hank tonight, but I did want to be with him. *When?*

As we rose from the table I said, "Hank, thank you for dinner. The thought of keeping my freedom and being released from this nightmare is wonderful, but overwhelming. I need a good night's sleep."

"No problem. Hey, let's stay an extra day. You don't have work tomorrow and I can take a day off. I'd love to show you the fun side of this town."

Too tired to think clearly, I said, "Sure."

***

By 10 AM Hank called to meet him in the lobby. I was ready, having shed the professional clothes used for the meetings to a tight, pink sleeveless sundress. The pink wedge sandals meant I could walk all day, if need be. It was a bright, blue sky 80-degree day.

I was glad I didn't sleep with Hank the night before, but my craving for him was growing. Was I desiring Hank because he saved me from prison? Or was this a real relationship? I had no idea about Hank's romantic past, so I was in no position to tell if he was faking his feelings for me just to get laid. It happens every day; I was wary.

Hank was standing in front of the elevator doors as they opened. "Good morning, Lauren. You look beautiful. We're going to have fun today," he said as he reached for my hand.

Off we went to a limousine. I guess Hank was busy planning last night.

"What are we doing today?" I asked.

"Lauren, we're going to the Hoover Dam first. It's out in the Mojave Desert, but we'll be there in less than an hour."

Hank opened the door, touched my arm and guided me into the vehicle. His gentle but strong touch woke up my desire for him.

Here we go, I thought. *Can I really do this?* I've known him and worked with him for years, but romantically, he seemed like a different person. Am I emotionally ready for a new man in my life? Probably not, but…

Chapter 11

As the morning wore on, the space between the two of us shrank, his frequent hugs and constant touching caused wetness between my legs. Hank put his arms around me and gazed into my eyes. I glanced at the outline of his rigid penis but didn't want to gawk.

We toured the Dam then Hank wanted to have lunch back in town. We went to the Picasso Restaurant at the Bellagio with windows looking out over the large fountain and a water show. After a few minutes in the restaurant, I realized we were the only patrons in the place.

"What good fortune," I said to Hank, "we are the only people here."

"I know," he responded, "this place is closed for lunch, so I called in a favor. We can dine with no interruptions."

"Hank, I'm flabbergasted, you opened a restaurant just to eat with me in privacy?"

"Yes." Hank put his hand on my thigh, almost the inside of my thigh.

I swallowed hard. His blue eyes were caressing my face with love and attention.

"Hank, what is going on here?"

"Lauren, I was attracted to you years ago, when I first met you. I was married, you were married, and the timing was off. I've been single for years, and now you are newly single – thank God! I'm not letting this relationship slip through my fingers. I want you."

"Hank, we barely know each other on a personal level."

"We've been working together for years. I do know you and love everything about you. You are what I want. You know me as well. Yes, it's on a professional basis, but I've been showing you my personal side since you and Victor broke up."

"Hank, I don't know. I've always thought of you as a business associate. A handsome one for sure, but a professional relationship."

"I know, but that's not how I've viewed you. You won't regret this. I'm not a hit and run type of man, at least not with you."

"Waiter," Hank raised his hand and ordered wine.

"I don't know what to say Hank."

"Don't worry; I am having a wonderful time with you and it seems that you are enjoying yourself as well."

I blushed. He was right.

The waiter appeared and opened a bottle of Caymus Conundrum. The cool, rich white wine on my tongue stimulated my oral senses. I could smell and almost taste Hank. Despite my hesitations, I wanted him. No doubt.

Lunch was spectacular, but it was hard to keep my mind on the food. I had sautéed black bass and Hank ordered Japanese Wagyu filet mignon. My body was tingling. I could feel the longing and heat between my legs grow.

We both sipped the wine and picked at our food. Hank had his hands all over me with his penis creating a tent in his pants. I was losing interest in lunch, my career and staying aloof. I wanted his hard, stiff love machine inside my wet pussy. And I needed it now.

Hank knew what he was doing to me. He rubbed his hand slowly, very slowly over the top of my thigh then he slipped his palm between my legs, caressing my inner thigh. I could barely breathe.

"Honey, let's go upstairs; I've longed for you. I'll touch and lick every part of you with our bodies moving as one, melting into each other in ecstasy," Hank said.

My thoughts went wild imagining Hank naked. His hands cupped my face, he kissed me gently, very slowly on the lips. He opened his mouth and rubbed his tongue on my teeth and then into my mouth. My body instinctively moved closer.

"Lauren, come with me to our room. I know you want me, don't be scared; this isn't a mistake. We need to be together – now," he whispered.

I drew in my breath and had trouble getting out of the chair.

He was right, it was time. He led me to his room, holding my hand. He was prepared for this moment. There were white roses on both nightstands by the bed, champagne and two crystal glasses by the couch and a beautiful white silk teddy laying on the bed.

"I'll bet you look great in that negligée, Hank," I kidded.

He smiled and said, "I can't wait to see you in this nightie. I've been imagining you in it since we arrived."

He walked over to me, put his arms around me and said, "I want you more than I've wanted anything in my entire life. I'll make you very happy today, we'll make each other very happy. I know it."

He started kissing and licking my neck. The desires for him shot through my body. I wanted to spread my legs and have him thrust his stiff rod inside my dripping box, but I let Hank lead.

Hank took my hand and led me to the bed. "I'm going to strip off your clothes. After I drink in your body with my eyes, I'm going to lick you everywhere. After you've come several times, I'm going to give you all of my love."

He pulled me into him, kissing me tenderly first on the lips, then all over my face. As he moved to my lips, his tongue entered my mouth in warm, slow strokes over my tongue. I wanted him inside me, but Hank, erect as he was, took his time.

He unzipped my dress, which fell to the floor. Hank stepped back, smiling and admiring my body. I was self-conscious, embarrassed and uncomfortable. My insecurities about my body were screaming in my head; paunchy stomach, thick thighs and what about my boobs?

"You are magnificent, my dear. I knew your body would be perfect." His smile and adoration made me feel secure.

"Hank, my body's not perfect, but thank you. Your words make me feel better."

Hank reached around me, undid my bra with a flick of his fingers and pulled it off. He immediately started kissing my breasts and nibbling the nipples. His hands were massaging my back. He kneeled and pulled off my panties.

He grinned at me, pushed me back on the bed, spread my legs apart and licked my stomach.

My heart was pounding with unsteady breathing and a pulsating pussy.

Hank's tongue was searing my skin as he licked my belly down to my pubic bone. He kissed my hipbones dragging his tongue to my upper thigh and then to the inside of my thighs.

"I can taste you, Lauren. You taste magnificent. I love your smell," he said as he kissed the inside of my thighs repeatedly. The kisses turned into leisurely lickings leading to my clitoris. I could have orgasmed, but I held back. I wanted to experience everything Hank had to offer. My body quivered in response to Hank's tongue in my crack.

He spread my lips with his fingers and put his entire mouth on my nerve center. As his tongue flicked my labia; it took every ounce of self-restraint not to have an orgasm.

"Oh Hank," I groaned, "This is better than any fantasy."

"I know honey, and it'll get better." he said looking up only for a few seconds.

Back to business, Hank ran his tongue across my clitoris to the inside of the thigh and slowly back to the other thigh. He paused in the center to nuzzle me. He kissed, sucked and licked me – everywhere.

He skillfully inserted a finger in my vagina while sucking my protrusion. He rubbed his finger along the walls causing my muscles to contract on him.

"Nice, you are so tight, I can't wait to enter you."

He pulled on my genitals with his mouth. That was it, I couldn't hold back any more.

I spread my legs farther apart, every muscle in my body tightened and the warm, loving sensation started. It moved through my body but seemed to get stronger with each passing moment as Hank continued thrilling me.

He didn't stop; I couldn't stop.

Every cell in my body was vibrating as Hank continued to kiss my inner thighs, suck my clitoris and rub his head in my groin. He took me to a heightened sense of pleasure I'd never experienced. Waves of joy emanated from my body.

"Lauren, you are so sensual, I have to enter you now before it's too late."

"Please," was all I could say.

Hank moved my whole body onto the bed and immediately found his way into my wet, throbbing vagina. I squeezed down on his largeness and we gyrated together with our hips in the air, Hank supporting himself with his hands, trying to get as much of himself into me as he could.

"Oh God, you feel stupendous, I never want to leave," Hank said.

"You're going to bring me to orgasm again, Hank. I can't help myself."

Hank continued to pump me.

"Lauren, I can't hold on anymore; I have to fill you with my love."

"Yes," was all I could murmur.

Chapter 12

With the pictures of Phil gambling and the accounting records of the amounts he gambled, he was caught red handed. The cash that was withdrawn from the Bermuda and Cayman accounts equaled the $22 MM stolen from the bank. In addition, there were pictures of Phil at both banks making the withdrawals.

"How could I be so stupid as to gamble in public?" Phil berated himself.

Yes sir, prison was where Phil was headed and for a long time. He was currently in a holding facility where inmates were housed before going to jail. The holding facilities have higher suicide rates than prisons as the newness of going away for years is enough to drive some to kill themselves.

There was one bright spot for Phil. He had the good sense to pay back his debt before he went on a spree. He was not safe, especially in jail, if he stilled owed that money. The spree ended early for Phil. He wanted to gamble all the money with the hopes that he would make enough money to live comfortably for the rest of his life. It didn't matter that $22 million was plenty of money for the rest of his life, anyone's life. His gambling addiction won. He gambled his life away.

Alone with his thoughts, Phil blamed and criticized everyone else for his life. He didn't acknowledge that it was his own poor choices that landed him in jail. He wanted to numb his emotions by gambling.

"Guard, I'm cold, please bring me another blanket," Phil begged.

"We provide only one blanket per prisoner, there are no goose down quilts or fluffy pillows available for the prisoners," the guard sneered.

"Do you want to flip a coin for an extra blanket?" Phil asked.

"You are pathetic," the guard replied.

Phil closed his eyes and thought of the loss of his wife, home, job, friends and the most crippling of all, his freedom to gamble.

Phil surveyed his cell, a small bar of soap, one flat pillow, a sheet turned gray and an itchy wool blanket. He closed his eyes, death seemed to be the only way out. He looked to the high ceiling with one light fixture. Was that fixture strong enough to hold a 185-pound man for a few minutes? He looked down and saw his leather shoelaces winding their way up his Sperry boat shoes.

Chapter 13

Fantasizing about Hank, I flew first class on my way home from Las Vegas. Yes, this trip was very different from my first trip to Sin City. I smelled Hank and felt his touch on my skin. We made love all afternoon and slept together that night. After more love in the morning, a shower and a limo ride to the airport, I was on a plane home. Hank stayed in Las Vegas.

Closing my eyes, I wondered, "What do I do now? Run from this relationship? Maybe Hank won't call. Am I interested or do I want out now before I get hurt again? The sex was the best I'd had in my life, but was it only for the moment? Would our enthusiasm die over the next few weeks or months?"

I called Greta from the cab on my way home.

"Hey, how are you? How's your business plan developing?" I asked.

"I'm making progress. I have a business proposal, some of the financials and a marketing plan spelled out. I'd love for you to review it. But how's your bank case going? I've been thinking of you."

"It's unbelievable. Phil is already behind bars. We have accounting evidence and video of Phil gambling. The trip to Las Vegas was very fruitful."

"That's great news! What a quick turnaround."

"Did I mention Hank Tofar? It was his escrow account that Phil robbed. He is a real estate developer and the bank's client."

"Yes."

"Hank and I went to Las Vegas and traced Phil's footsteps. Hank had Vegas contacts and single handedly solved this case. Phil is in a holding cell."

"That's great news! Congrats. He helped you with this case? I'd say that's Helping with a capital "H". What happened out there?"

"Can't get anything by you, Greta. We got together. It was earth shattering. I want more, but I'm not sure how much I'll see him or should see him. I'm confused, that's for sure."

"I'm so happy for you. You probably won't be working at your bank anyway, how about just having fun? Can you meet me at another Al-Anon meeting? We have lots to discuss."

"Sounds great, I'll be at the meeting tonight, you going there?"

"Yes, see you there."

As soon as I hung up, Hank called. I smiled.

"Hi Hank, I just landed. I'm on my way home."

"Glad you are home safely. I can't stop thinking about you. I'm flying to Manhattan in two days, can I see you?"

"Sure, when do you want to meet?"

"Lauren, I want to see you the whole time. Let's see the city through a whole new set of eyes. I want to be with you. I'm not in this for the sex, although now that we've had it; I'm consumed thinking about our next encounter."

"Hank, I'm nervous about getting in another dysfunctional relationship."

"I understand; it's scary for me too. I have a suite at the Mandarin Oriental Hotel. Pack a bag for four days and come join me. No pressure, if it doesn't work, we'll part friends. If we have a nice time; let's meet again."

I liked his attitude.

"Also, we need to discuss your career. What do you want to do next?" he asked.

"I'm thinking I'll have to leave the financial industry; even though I don't want to. While I can keep my certifications because I'll be exonerated, the news of the robbery will follow me. I think it'll be hard to get a job; maybe I could do something to help women. I have a friend who wants to open a haven for abused women."

"Oh, that's interesting, helping women, but I have a few ideas. You're meeting me at the hotel, yes? It's important for us to see each other regularly, especially in the beginning of our relationship."

"We're in a relationship, are we Hank?" I teased.

"Oh, I just meant…"

"It's okay, Hank. Thanks for your help. I'm looking forward to your visit. See you in two days."

Chapter 14

Schlepping to the west side, I went to this Al-Anon meeting with hope in my heart. As soon as I walked into the room, I spotted Greta, she moved her purse and I sat next to her.

She gave me a big grin and said, "Great to see you. Can we get a bite after the meeting?"

"Sure."

She turned to me to talk, but the meeting started. We shrugged our shoulders, winked and started listening.

The topic was relationships, making the most of your personal interactions. I couldn't believe how relevant the topic was. As it turns out, discussing pertinent topics happens frequently in 12-step programs. People have similar problems even though I always feel unique. The hamster wheel of my mind is a scary place and keeps me special. But the truth is: I'm not so different from others, after all.

We considered honesty and forgiveness in relationships. Two topics Victor and I did not discuss. He had been lying to me for years about his cheating and drinking. Yet he still blamed me for his problems. Forgiveness was not in his vocabulary; he was estranged from his brother, friends and other family members. I was determined to make forgiveness part of my life. I didn't want to carry grudges or resentments. I needed to be free of the past: mistakes, angers and all. It was time to learn how to handle problems maturely. Forgiving Victor and Phil was on top of my to-do list.

When I lost focus, I fantasized about Hank at the Al-Anon meeting. What was this man doing to me? Could this relationship really be as fulfilling in the long run as it seemed right now?

After the meeting Greta said, "Let's go to the diner. We can talk there."

"Okay."

***

I ordered the Cobb salad with oil and vinegar on the side; Greta ordered a cheeseburger with fries.

"You look totally different. That trip to Vegas really worked wonders. Relief from jail time clearly is part of your improved looks but could Hank be responsible for the glow?" Greta said.

"I can't believe how different I feel after only a few days in Vegas."

"Have you started working this program? Are you reading and writing daily? Did you find a sponsor?"

"No, I don't have a sponsor yet, but I've been reading Courage to Change and writing sporadically. As I said, it was a fruitful trip; my boss is already behind bars. It took the bank exactly three hours to charge him after we produced the evidence. I couldn't have done it by myself. I owe a big debt of gratitude to Hank. He knew who to talk to and where to go. Because of Hank's connections, we have Phil's gambling records. He's going away for a long time and I'm a free woman. What a relief."

"Nice," Greta said, "that was a quick resolution to a major problem."

"Yeah, but it didn't seem quick while I was going through it. What's going on with you?"

"My boss hit on me. I rejected him. He's pissed."

"Just for saying no?"

"Yes, I'm sure the female employees always said yes to him. He threatened to fire me within 30 seconds of no coming out of my mouth."

"Oh shit, sorry Greta."

"What really annoys me is that he hits on the ladies at the call center all the time and gets laid frequently. How offensive is one "no" from me? I'm only one of many. He doesn't pay for their sexual favors, but clearly if they don't participate in his plans, the ladies fear they might lose their jobs. How disgusting is that?"

Greta continued, "I feel that saying no is within my right, especially as far as he is concerned. But, Lauren, I still have shame that he propositioned me. In fact, I regret the past mistakes I've made with men. If I said yes to the boss; it would only be another mistake."

"You are right, Greta, you did the right thing by saying no."

"I need to work this program: forgive myself, maybe even love myself," Greta lamented. "I will look at my character defects and ask my Higher Power for the power to change. Women need a place to go if they are being used or abused. I need to create a comfortable, safe environment for women where they can openly talk about the abuse, the abuser and problems with no shame or risk of retaliation."

"I love that idea, Gretz," I said.

"I'm working on finding a place and looking into grants for funding."

"Good luck, Greta," I said. "I can help you. I analyze new business proposals frequently and help people with funding, if possible."

"Thanks for your offer. As I move forward, I'll keep you posted."

"I'm happy to help, Greta; women need to stick together. You probably won't make enough money at your agency to pay employees and make monthly loan payments, but maybe your grant idea will help you fund an agency for battered ladies. Have you managed this type of organization?"

"Yes, I ran a clinic in southern Jersey for ladies. It's shocking to realize how often women put up with abuse."

"Great, that experience will help you know how to set up shop, run your own organization and get funding."

"I appreciate your council and time," Greta said.

Chapter 15

Nervously I walked into the hotel and looked for Hank. I was on time, but I didn't know if Hank was punctual. Damn, there was so much I didn't know about him. It was 10 AM and I didn't even know if Hank just arrived in NYC or spent the night at the hotel.

As soon as I fretted, I saw Hank's smile. He was charging across the lobby.

"Lauren, you are right on time, wonderful. I'm so glad you are here; been thinking about you since Las Vegas."

"Me too, Hank."

"I have a room for us. Do you want to freshen up and drop off your bags before we explore Manhattan?"

Hank was modest, the room was a penthouse suite lavishly decorated and loaded with flowers, fruit, and wines.

"Hank, this is extravagant. I don't know what to say."

"Don't worry, Lauren, no pressure. I was frugal my entire life; now I want to enjoy myself with someone special and that someone is you."

I smiled. "Right, no pressure,"

He moved over to me with a prowling animal look on his face. His eyes stared deep into me. He put his arms around me and whispered into my ear, "I want you right here, right now. I want to love you and then go out exploring. We'll both be more relaxed and enjoy the city if we connect immediately."

"I want you too," was all I could say.

He nuzzled my neck, hands squeezing my ass. I put my arms around him and brought him closer to me. I could feel his rigid penis poking me. I started massaging it through his pants.

"Oh, baby, I love it when you touch me. Don't stop," Hank moaned.

He had my top off before the next breath. He unbuttoned my pants, slide his hand down my front and was stimulating my clit. My body shuddered to his touch.

I undid his pants, pulled them down, kneeled and put his engorged cock in my mouth. Slowly, I ran my mouth up and down his shaft, then taking the whole thing into my mouth I flicked my tongue on the underside of his penis, especially at the tip.

"Oh my God Lauren, I want to explode in your mouth, but I need to go inside of your juicy pussy first."

"You can explode all over me, I love your saltiness."

"You talk dirty; I love it. I'll fill you up with my love. Off your knees, I need to excite your crack and slip my manliness into you."

Moaning with Hank's every stroke over my clitoris I was soon ready for my vagina to clamp down on him and he didn't deny me.

He knew exactly where my craving cavity was located and inserted his outsized erection in me. There was no fumbling or missing the mark for Hank, he knew exactly how to enter me.

Our hips moved in unison, he nuzzled his head into my neck and started licking the base of my collar. My dripping pussy clamped onto him.

"Oh, honey, that is perfect. I've never felt a woman squeeze so hard on my cock; you are driving me into oblivion."

***

After a quick shower, Hank and I sauntered out of the hotel to be bombarded with horns, cars, people and music from Columbus Circle. Quite a contrast to the elegant, quiet digs we just left.

"Let's walk through Central Park and shop on Madison Avenue once we get to the east side," Hank said.

The problem: I was short on cash (no job) but didn't want to be a killjoy. So, I said, "Sounds like fun."

It was fun. Hank knew the Central Park concept was discussed in the 1850s and completed in 1873. No two bridges were the same. The park was designed by Frederick Law Olmstead and Calvert Vaux. Hank showed me the only remaining survey bolt from John Randel, Jr., the park's surveyor. The bolt is embedded in rock just north of the 65th Street. The park survived several eras with little funding, but always staged a comeback. Currently, there are over 40 million visitors a year in Central Park. I live in Manhattan and didn't know Central Park's history.

Hank stopped a few times to kiss me on a bridge, under a tree or by the beautiful Bethesda Fountain Plaza. He didn't let go of my hand.

"Lauren, I am so happy you agreed to stay with me. Your presence makes this trip worthwhile. Tomorrow I have one business meeting with your former employer. I'm thinking about moving my account to City Bank. I called and talked to the head of private clients at City yesterday. He is interested in hiring you."

"Really great news, Hank. You must have some serious pull with him. I don't know how to thank you."

"I can think of a few ways."

"Very funny. I don't know what I want to do. I couldn't cover your account anymore. Besides, I'm not sure it's appropriate anyway."

"Why not? I told the bank we have a personal relationship, so there are no secrets to keep."

"Hmm, I'll have to think about that, but I'd love to meet with your contact and see what they have in mind and what the opportunity looks like."

"No problem. I'll arrange for your meeting to take place while I meet with your former employer. This way we'll have simultaneous meetings and we can spend more time together. If you want, we can review your career opportunity together, but it's your decision; I don't want to pry."

"That arrangement sounds perfect," I said.

As we turned the corner onto Madison Avenue, I smelled perfume coming from Bond No. 9 boutique off 72nd Street. The aroma brought a smile to my face.

"Want to get some perfume? I'd love to smell several different scents on you," Hank said.

"Sure," I said, worried about the prices.

"I want to buy you two or three different scents, so you have a perfume that fits your mood," Hank said.

I wondered if he knew I was concerned about the money. Hank squeezed my hand and smiled at me. How could he know?

After Hank bought two perfumes that I loved, he suggested we go to Emilio Pucci Ltd.

I had never been in the store. It looks expensive from the outside. Only a few elegant dresses on display, a rack of little black dresses, a few accessories and lots of marble, brass and empty space. With Manhattan rents so high, abundant space in a retail shop means serious dollars for the merchandise. Hank seemed right at home in the shop; I felt out of place and awkward.

Hank walked over to the salesclerk and said he wanted to see a few cocktail dresses for me. I smiled demurely, blushing.

She smiled and said, "No problem, it looks like you are a size 8. Is that correct?"

I was shocked she knew my size just by looking at me, but as I would learn that day, this woman was a pro.

"Hank, I don't have any black-tie affairs to go to; I don't know if I'll ever use the dress."

"Yes, you will. I go to charity fundraisers all the time. You'll need several dresses. The same crowd attends many of these events and I know women don't like to wear the same outfit," he smiled.

I smiled at his sensitivity and felt a longing between my legs.

The pro showed up with five beautiful dresses and said, "I'll bet these all look great on you. Let's go to the dressing room."

"Hey, I want to see each one on you," Hank requested.

"No problem."

In the dressing room, the clerk told me to take off everything but my panties. I complied. She helped me with the first dress by reaching down the top and pulling up each breast. I was shocked at her familiarity, but the dressed looked better with that assistance.

Hank's expression made all my apprehension disappear when I emerged from the dressing room. He had lust in his eyes. He walked over and pulled me to him. I could feel his cock getting hard and his breathing quicken. He put his hands in my hair and whispered in my ear, "We'll go to a restaurant where you can wear this dress tonight. I want to explode all over you."

The dress was pale pink with mesh covering the back and the shoulders. I couldn't wear a bra, but the stiff chiffon held the breasts in place and appeared to slim the waist, which, in my mind, was a good thing. The bottom of the dress was a straight skirt ending just above the knee. Thankfully, there was a long slit in the back, so walking was possible.

Hank bought four dresses. He got hard each time I appeared from the dressing room. I couldn't help but feel sexy in the extravagance he was showing me.

After leaving the store, Hank whispered, "I know you're hungry, but we have to get a cab. It's time to caress and lick you again. I want to be inside of you."

I smiled.

Was this relationship real?

***

Back at the hotel, Hank started kissing my neck in the elevator. I felt the heat between my legs and wanted his hand there.

As we walked down the hall to our room, Hank had his arm around me forcibly grabbing my waist and not letting go. He was breathing heavily and focused on the door to our room at the end of the hall. It was a long hall.

Inside, he immediately turned to me with a big smile and let out a sigh.

"Lauren, I am going make you very happy this afternoon. After I remove your clothes, I am going to rub oil all over your body. This will be the finest massage of your life."

I didn't have the heart to tell him there was competition for the best massage. While Brett wasn't on my mind much since Las Vegas, I suspected I would see Brett again.

Hank put his arms around me, undid my dress and bra. He was walking me to the bedroom before I realized he was fully clothed. I reached out to unbutton his shirt, but Hank moved my hands away from his body.

"I want your full attention on my hands, Lauren. I need an hour to touch, rub and caress you before you stroke me. You need to feel my love."

He gently laid me on the bed, took off his button-down shirt with a white T-shirt underneath exposing his muscular arms and abs.

"You are luscious. I can't take my eyes off you," he said as reached down to me with his oiled hands. He flipped me onto my stomach.

"Let's start with your back," he said as he straddled me just below my ass. His hands grabbed my butt as he pushed down hard moving his hands out to my hips, spreading my cheeks.

He leaned over and whispered, "I want all of you honey."

I gulped, never a fan of anal sex. I hoped he wanted to be in my pussy, but did Hank have a special touch to make anal sex enjoyable? Doubtful but…*maybe* s*omeday.*

Hank's hands moved from the butt to the lower back, up the back on each side of the spine around the shoulders and down the arms. As he got up to the shoulders, I could feel his hot breath on the back of my neck.

"Your back is beautiful, I have to come on it sometime soon, but not right now. This is your time."

Hank massaged me like a pro. He didn't ask for permission to touch me intimately; he was in charge and clearly not to be denied. After he massaged the back and the upper legs, including the inner thighs, he flipped me over and kissed my lips. His warm breath and lusty stare caused me to squirm.

He spent a long time rubbing my thighs. Every stroke went from my knee to my vagina. He circled the clitoris several times and went down the other leg, slowly massaging the thigh down to the knee. I could feel wetness seeping out from my pussy.

My breathing deepened, I wanted to come, but Hank knew when I was on the edge and slowed his stroke. He didn't touch my clitoris until I regained my composure.

He moved up to my breasts. He sucked, blew and gently bit my nipples. They stiffened in response to his caresses. My chest started heaving.

"No, honey, you're not coming yet. I want to touch, lick and rub every cell of your body before you come. When you explode, I'm going to be right here driving you to an ecstasy you have never experienced. I'm going to take you to the brink of an orgasm then ease off and start you up again until I determine it's time."

"I don't know if I can refrain from coming, Hank. Your touch sends me to orbit," I said.

"You will Lauren, I'll make sure."

Hank was right, despite my squirms and protests; he backed off as soon as I was ready to pop. I couldn't come, but Hank didn't stop massaging. My senses were on overdrive.

He grabbed my calf muscles so hard I thought I'd cramp, but instead a euphoric, calmness started in my lower legs, spreading to my entire body. Hank squeezed my thigh muscles firmly, rubbed the hips and the glutes, up the side of my stomach to my shoulders. I felt surrounded by his love. In a cocoon, safe and protected by his warm energy. I melted.

He saw I was relaxed and took action to change the calmness. His fingers tickled my inside thighs eventually converging on my clit. He softly rubbed the outside of my lips and the crease between the legs. My head started swooning, I lost track of time.

He slipped his fingers between my lips, I wanted to explode. Hank whispered in my ear, "Soon baby, very soon. Enjoy this touch."

Two fingers rubbed me from the top of the labia down into my pussy and back to the sensitive button. He didn't stop but moved slowly. I'd never felt such a long stimulating stroke. Between the stimulation for the clit and delving into my pussy where my muscle clamped down on his two fingers, I was where Hank wanted me to be: desperately craving an explosion.

"Do it, honey, I want to see you writhe in ecstasy showing me how you come. I want to see your joy."

Those words set a chain reaction in my body that couldn't be stopped. Hank didn't stop either. He circled my clit repeatedly. My back arched, nipples stiffened and muscles in my vagina contracted. Warmth and love spread through my sweaty body with all the cells tingling. I had no idea how long I stayed in this state.

Hank didn't stop rubbing my bundle of nerves until I said, "No more, please."

He let me catch my breath and then started kissing my face.

"I love you," he said.

"Hank, I don't know what to say. That was the best massage I've ever had," ignoring the "L" word he just uttered.

"Yes, and this is just the start of our fun Lauren." He rolled on top of me.

He was so stiff his largeness pressed into my belly. I smiled to myself and knew I wanted to taste his salty deliciousness.

I reached down to pull his pants off, but Hank had them off before I got there. His cock looked luscious. Hard, red and did I see throbbing? I put it in my mouth.

"Oh. God," he breathed.

As I slowly went down on his cock, rubbing my tongue on the underside of his penis and around the tip, he said, "Stop. I'm going to come way too fast."

He pulled me off, pushed me on the bed and climbed on top of me. He inserted his penis inside my wet red velvet and I clamped down on him.

"Augh, I am so hot for you." He exhaled.

I thrust my hips into his and he started rhythmically pulling and inserting his rod.

His tongue flowed into my mouth.

"I want to be totally inside all of you," Hank snorted.

As we moved in unison, I could tell he was trying not to come.

"Hank, I know you want to explode in my hot box, go ahead."

"No, I want you to come with me, I know you have one more orgasm in you."

He reached down and rubbed my clitoris. Feeling the heat from his hand deepened my breathing with my heart pounding louder and faster.

"Hank, I can cum with you."

"Soon, honey, not yet."

He rolled over so I was on top. With his hands on my hips his lusty eyes looked up at me.

"You are magnificent with my big dick inside of you. Your body is perfect, ride me baby."

I started slowly riding his staff, increasing the speed slightly with each stroke.

I grabbed my breasts and squeezed them.

"Oh, that's perfect baby; don't stop. I'm filling you up with my love."

"Don't stop," was all I could say as the primal release started between my legs and vibrated throughout my body.

Chapter 16

"Lauren, I'm outside the office of your former CEO. He wants to thank me for getting the evidence to put Phil away for many years," Hank said.

"I owe you a thank you as well. You saved me from jail and, depending how my interview goes today, I could be working soon," I said.

"No thank you is necessary. Your love and attention are all I want and more than I can handle sometimes."

"You seem to be handling things very well. I appreciate everything you've done for me, thank you."

Sitting in the waiting room of City Bank's head of Private Banking stirred up the desire to go back to work. Elegant furniture, oriental rugs, people walking with purpose, phones ringing softly in the background and the hushed tones of people talking about building wealth all combined to remind me of the highlights of my career. It was time to focus on my profession.

I met with Paul Tannery, the head of Private Wealth division at City Bank. He asked about the robbery and how it was resolved. I provided him with the details of Phil's gambling problem, being found in Las Vegas and landing in jail.

"I still don't know how he got my signature on the release form," I said.

"That's sounds like a problem for your former employer," Paul said.

"Yes, but I learned a valuable lesson. I must listen to my intuition when things don't seem right; even if it is my boss. I always processed the forms, not Phil. I need to be careful when the situation isn't quite right."

"What do you want to do for your next career move?" he asked.

"I would like to be a private banker, helping wealthy families and growing small to mid-sized businesses," I said.

"What accounts do you think you could bring into the bank? Aside from Hank Tofar, of course."

I was prepared for this question. I rattled off my top six accounts that I thought would transfer their assets to City Bank. I kept in touch with all my accounts during the suspension. I also let them know when Phil was behind bars and I was exonerated. A few key clients said they would follow me to a new firm. All of them expressed their support for me. The question is just how far did that support go? Transferring assets is inconvenient at best; at worst, it's a nightmare.

"Well, Lauren, we are interested in hiring you. Your salary is $125,000, plus commission. You'll have an expense account, we have a travel agency to help you with planning your travel, a matching 401K plan and a great medical plan. Are you interested?"

I smiled. The base was almost 20% more than my last job and it sounded as if the perks were better.

"What is the commission structure for the different products?" I asked.

"I'll have my secretary give you a copy of our remunerations and benefits. Please take a day or two and let us know by Friday if you are interested in joining us. Here's my card. Give me a call if you have any questions about this opportunity. If you decide to join us, I'll send out an offer letter that day."

"Thank you, Paul." I was floored. This was my easiest job interview, but knew it was Hank's influence. I didn't want the job only because Hank's assets were coming with me; I wanted to prove my worth. Could I do it?

Walking out to the street with blue skies, a cool breeze and the bumps from people walking in a rush, I felt exhilarated, and grateful. Was I taking the easy way by accepting this job? *Maybe.*

The earning potential thrilled me, but I was hitching my star to Mr. Tofar. Did I want my career successes to be connected to my personal relationship with Hank? That answer was no.

I wondered how Hank's meeting was going. I was sure my meeting was shorter.

Sauntering in midtown, I went into a coffee shop to call Greta. I liked her; she saw right through my smoke screens. She had a well-developed intuition, refreshingly direct approach and wanted to establish a place for abused women. Her working at the call center was only a pit stop for her and not her long-term career path, especially with a menacing boss.

"Hey Gretz, Lauren here. How are you?"

"I haven't seen you for a few days, everything okay?"

"Yes, Hank is in town and we're staying in a hotel, playing tourist for a few days."

"What fun! How's the old man treating you?"

"He's unbelievable. Aside from solving my theft problem, he got me an interview today and they offered me a job."

"That's great news!"

"Yes, but Hank's assets have to come to the bank with me. So now my career is tied to this man – forever."

"Forever is a long time, Lauren. If you are asking, take the job, bring in lots of new clients and when you and Hank run your course, you'll have plenty of business from other sources. I will say, though, Hank seems like a keeper, that's for sure."

"Thanks, Gretz. I appreciate your input. What's going on with you?"

"Nothing as exciting as a new man and job."

"Well, that doesn't happen every day," I said.

"My boss asked me to stay after work for a drink – again. I said no – again. I don't know why he won't take no for an answer. I think it is past time for a new job, so I've been working on the proposal."

"Meanwhile, you might want to work at a place that helps battered women. That could help you with additional ideas to run your own place."

"Wonderful idea, I know three people who work at that type of agency. I'll bet one of them would hire me or at least let me volunteer there."

"It'll add to your experience and help you learn where the local contacts and landmines are."

"Let's meet after Hank leaves town."
"Perfect, I'll call when he is gone."

Chapter 17

Racing across town to the Al-Anon meeting, it occurred to me that I had not told Hank about my involvement in a 12-step program. Wondering how he would react caused me a moment of concern, but given how accepting Hank is, I hoped it wouldn't be a problem for him.

Walking into the meeting, Greta waved me over and I took the seat next to her.

We hugged.

"Hey, how are you?" I asked.

"Great, contacted one of my acquaintances about working at her women's organization and I'm meeting her tomorrow for an interview. Let's go to the deli after the meeting. I'm starving and dreaming about a hot pastrami."

Smiling, I said, "Glad things are moving along, Gretz. Are your finances okay to work in this type of industry? You know it is not the highest paying industry."

"No, my finances are weak, but I have to follow my heart. My mom wants me to pursue more education and become a tenured teacher, but I feel a calling to this work. Certainly, working at a call center with a predator as a boss isn't working for me."

"You have to follow your heart. Maybe this program will help you with your relationship with your Mom."

"That would be a relief," Greta said. "Meanwhile, would you take a look at my business plan?"

"Yes, definitely. We have to find sources of money, as well as, contracts with government organizations that will pay you for your services to help women."

After quickly reviewing a well thought out business plan, with sensible revenue and expense forecasts I had to say I was impressed with Greta's ability. She didn't include insurance costs, but that seemed to be the only missing expense.

The meeting started, I put down the paperwork. The leader talked about the pain of living with an addict; the hostile, resentful and belligerent attitude – the craziness. I identified with him; Victor's anger was always just below the surface, ready to explode, especially when we were alone. When we were out with friends, Victor appeared charming and fun loving; but he was off to my trained eye.

Greta looked sad; I knew she was thinking about her ex too.

After the meeting, I said, "Dinner time?"

"Great."

"What is your end game here, Gretz? Do you want to expand, assuming you are a success or sell the business?"

"Good question. I want to grow by establishing safe environments for women throughout the tristate area. Initially, we won't have the funds to buy a building in each borough, New Jersey and Connecticut; but we can establish meetings to be held in hospitals, churches or schools. The first safe home should be in Manhattan; the lower east side or Harlem might be in our price range. We'll be able to reach women in the City. I'd be happy if we can start by helping 20 women. You know, abused women come from all socio-eco, ethnic and religious backgrounds. No group has a monopoly on poor behavior toward women."

She continued, "Maybe we will be lucky enough to have a building donated to us. There are municipalities that provide buildings to our type of entity and I know government agencies that would pay for our services once we establish a program. Also, perhaps I could get some funding from hospitals and nonprofits, but that usually works if you have signed contracts with the government. I don't think banks or financial institutions would support me just yet."

"You're right. Once you have a predictable cash flow, you might be able to get a loan from a bank, but you must show a profit large enough to cover the loan payment. For the moment, we can turn to foundations that help abused women for financial support."

"We'll need to determine where all the funds will come from before we finalize your business plan. This means we must know the exact amount that you need to start your business. I recommend you find your location first. You don't want visible retail space and that will keep costs lower," I said.

"Also, don't forget to determine how much money you need to cover your living costs," I added.

"Ugh, I haven't thought of paying myself. Thank you, would you consider being my partner? I'd love to have you as a partner or on my board."

"Hmm, let me think about that offer. I'll be working soon and may not have the time. Can I get back to you next week? You might want to have a lawyer, an accountant and a local politician or two on your board."

"Makes sense, but I could use your expertise and insights, Lauren."

"I'm always there for you, Greta," I said.

Chapter 18

"Hi Lauren, God, I miss you. I wish I was next to you, kissing your neck and unbuttoning your pants."

Hank at his finest; his lust for me always brought a smile to my face. It had been a week since his four-day visit to NYC. I missed him too.

"It's great to hear from you. How are things going down in Florida?"

"Okay, but I wish you could be here with me. You start your job at City next week. Any chance you can catch a shuttle to Miami until Sunday?"

"Hank sounds like a great idea. See you soon."

***

The length from the gate to outside the Miami airport where Hank was waiting was long. The moving walkways crept slowly, and people blocked me from passing them. The agitation disappeared quickly when I saw his smile. He was in a white Infiniti Q80 Inspiration. It was a sleek white sports car with a black back window that formed a "V". A two-door car with the irresistible smell of new leather started my thinking about sex with him in the car. With not much room for activities, I assumed Hank didn't want to christen his car, but I was wrong.

"Hi honey," Hank said, "I hope you like my new car."

"It's a masterpiece, Hank. Did you just buy it?"

"Yes, we have to break her in. We're going to the Everglades; we'll have some privacy there."

"Privacy for what Hank?" I teased.

He stuck his tongue out and gave me a wink. My cheeks flushed; vibrations pulsed between my legs. Yes, I knew what was on Hank's mind; I just didn't know the details.

After we drove for over an hour, we were surrounded by flat land, water, and low vegetation. We were alone in the Everglades.

"We are some distance from the park entrance, but I know a secluded road about five miles from here. It'll be a perfect viewing spot for your first experience in the Everglades," Hank said. I was sure he didn't mean viewing Mother Nature but rather Hank Tofar.

I leaned over and kissed him slowly and tenderly in the crevice between his neck and his collarbone. Loving the power of a simple kiss, I could see Hank stiffen. He pressed down on the gas pedal. I felt the power surge through the car into my groin.

He made a sharp right turn onto a gravel road with lots of low-lying trees, bushes and grasses blocking anyone's view; just in case anyone happen to stumble across this part of the Everglades. After a few hundred yards, he turned right into an open patch of dirt and grass and turned to me with a wide grin.

"I've been thinking about how to have some fun with you in this car. I came up with a few ideas. Do you want to hear them, or should I show you?"

What's a girl to do? I wasn't sure which to pick when Hank got out of the car and came over to my side. He opened my door, grabbed my thighs and swung them toward him, spreading my legs. He put his hand between my legs, rubbing up and down. He leaned in and kissed me hard. Clearly, we were going with the showing option.

"We have to get these pants off you, now," he panted. "I realize this is a new car, but part of me wants your pussy juice on this leather seat, so I can smell you every time I get in the car."

"That's flattering, but I don't want to be the one to kill that luxurious new car smell," I said.

"Lean back, these pants have got to go," he demanded.

As soon as the pants were off, he dove between my legs, put my thighs over his shoulders and swirled his tongue on my clitoris. Between the sun's rays warming me, the smell of the outdoors, the leather, and grunts of heron, his passion was irresistible. I lifted my hips off the seat and felt pussy juice run down my back.

Feeling like I was going to come too soon, I pleaded, "Hank, I really want your rock-hard cock inside me."

"Sure," he stood up, pulled me up by my arms, moved me to the back of car and bent me over the "V" shaped back window.

He was inside of me before my footing was stable. As I lost my balance, he grabbed my hips and said "I gotcha, you're not going anywhere."

After he penetrated me, he started slowly withdrawing his stiff shaft just to the end, but before taking it out, he pushed himself into me – as far as he could go. The slow pace helped me regain my composure, but I could feel his cock engorging as the muscles in my vagina gripped him with each withdrawal. The rays from the sun encased us in a warm lover's embrace.

Reaching around me with his right arm, his hand landed between my legs. He alternated between tickling the inside of my thighs and playing with the outside of the lips. This was followed by his fingers twirling around my joy spot. With his penis gliding inside of me and my clitoris stimulated I lost track of myself, focusing only on the sensations of my body.

Hank whispered in my ear, "you are so wet, you make my cock rock hard. I want to explode inside of you right now, but I'm going to wait. I want to climax with you in the car."

"How can we come together inside the car?"

"I'll show you, in a minute, but this feels so good, I don't want to stop," he said.

After grabbing my breasts from behind and burying his face in my hair and the back of my neck, he said, "I can't leave this position. I want you."

His right hand moved from my breasts down to my clitoris. He started circling my nerves which opened the lips and caused my juice to drip on his hand and the car.

"Oh Lauren, I can't stop. Squeeze my shaft hard, your juice is all over my cock and dripping onto my balls, I'm going to explode inside of you."

"Don't stop Hank; I'm cumming."

Chapter 19

"Welcome to City Bank, Lauren. This is where your office is located. Your desk is stocked with all the office supplies you'll need. My name is Joanna. I'm here to put through your trades, make sure they settle properly, follow up on asset transfers and help you any way possible."

"Thanks, Joanna," I responded.

My first day at work. I was so happy and relieved to be working in my favorite field. So many calls to make, processes and systems to learn, I didn't know where to start – so I called Hank.

"Hi Hank, you are my first call. How are you?"

"Lauren, congratulations on your new job. I know you'll be a huge success and happy at City Bank."

"Thanks honey. I'm a little intimidated right now. What are you doing?"

"I'm thinking about you and touching myself."

"Nice, Hank."

"Lauren, I'd like to celebrate your first day with you tonight."

"Thanks, Hank, but can you get up here by dinner time?" I asked.

"I'm leaving soon. I have a flight at 1 PM. I'm not sure if this is too forward, but I'd love to stay with you at your home tonight. What do you think? I could book a hotel room, but I'd rather nest with you in your surroundings."

"That sounds great, Hank. You are welcomed in my place, but thanks for asking. I don't want to live with anyone, but a visit sounds great."

"I hear you, Lauren, but I hate to hear you talking negatively about our future. First, I'm not Victor, his addiction was my gain. Also, I'm not moving in, just staying with you when I'm in town, but let's see how this visit goes before we discuss anything else. It is your apartment, not mine."

"That sounds more than reasonable and, as of now, you are most welcomed. Meanwhile, when can I start transferring your assets to City Bank?"

"That's one of the many things I love about you, Lauren, you don't beat around the bush. You are direct and honest; it is an uplifting change. Send me the documents, I'll sign them, and you can start the transfer."

"Okay, I'll have the documents to you today or tomorrow at the latest. Thanks, Hank."

"Hey, am I providing you with enough physical love? Do you feel loved?"

"Yes, why are you asking?"

"I just want to keep you happy, if you are longing for more touch, please let me know. It probably means I'm not visiting you enough, so let me know if that happens. I'll be on the next flight."

"Hank, I'm seeing you tonight and I left Miami yesterday. I'm seeing you plenty, thank you."

Dinner was lovely, but after Hank went back to Miami the next morning, things got rough.

Chapter 20

"What, he's dead? How can that be?" I asked with my heart pounding and breathe shortening.

"Phil Longines hung himself; wrapped his head with the bed sheet and used his shoe laces to string himself up in the holding cell. I've never seen anything like it," said the deputy.

"When did this happen?" I gasped.

"Two days after he arrived in the holding cell."

"Why are you calling me now?"

"Phil left you a note. I wanted to send it to you, but it took me some time to locate you. Your former bank wouldn't give me your address, so hence the call. I'm sorry to give the news over the phone. Were you close with Phil?"

"No," I snapped, "he set me up for his robbery."

"Oh, sorry to hear that. Do you want me to send you his note?"

"Yes, thank you. My address is 182 East 75 St. Apt. 2B NYC, NY 10021," I said cringing.

What could Phil possibly want to say to me after his suicide? Guilt and remorse set in.

"Damn it," I thought to myself.

"Why should I feel bad? He's the one who robbed the bank, set me up as the fall guy, gambled away millions of dollars and mocked me once he was caught and still thought he was home free."

Why do I need to be liked by everyone? Why do I take on other people's problems? I can't help other people and they don't want my help anyway. Phil's a creep and it's not my fault that he is dead, I thought.

I realized it was time to go to an Al-Anon meeting. Life and outside circumstances were negatively impacting me. I wanted peace. *Why can't I accept life as it comes, why do I resist events I can't control? Phil's dead and that's that.*

I'm done worrying about others. I can only change me and my beliefs, I thought. I'm staying in the day with my problems, my behaviors and my thoughts. There is nothing I could have done for him. Perhaps Al-Anon was changing me.

I called Hank; he didn't pick up. Off to work I went.

***

Finally, Hank called.

"Lauren, I just found out Phil committed suicide. You are not responsible, you know."

"Thanks for calling, Hank, I know it's not on my shoulders, but I am sad he felt desperate enough to kill himself. Plus, he was my boss for 4 ½ years. It is a loss. Did you know he wrote me a note? The Sheriff sent it to me, but I haven't received it yet."

"What could he possibly want to say to you?" Hank said breathlessly.

"I don't know. We weren't close at work. As you know, he was busy with racing forms and not focusing on our clients or his employees."

"Please call me once you receive the note. I'd be interested in what he has to say. What are you wearing?"

"Very funny, I'm at work."

"Do you want to go the ladies' room or outside for a private conversation?"

"You are a hound dog, my friend. I need to stay focused on work, but thanks for the interest. We'll have phone sex another time."

"I'll be in the City in two days. You free?"

"Are you coming north for business or me? I don't remember you being in town this much when I covered you from my previous employer."

"Okay, you got me. Let's talk tonight? I want to tell you a bedtime story."

"I'm sure you do."

Why was Hank so concerned about the contents of Phil's note?

***

One day later the letter from Phil was waiting for me at the front desk when I got home. Trembling, I stared at the letter from the Sheriff's department.

What could Phil possibly have to say to me from his grave?

Heart pounding, halting breath and damp skin all added to make thinking difficult.

I retreated to my co-op and locked the door behind me, but the lock didn't keep my fears out. I thought about my Al-Anon program – I couldn't control Phil, especially from the grave. Whatever he had to say was about him, not me. I know I did the right thing. I did not steal the money from the bank. I looked in my heart and saw a small amount of confidence, but a large amount of terror and anxiety. Get it together, Lauren.

I fumbled opening the letter.

Lauren,

Hank and I set you up for the bank robbery. We wanted to split the money. I needed it, so I could continue to gamble. Sitting in this cell, I can't believe the audacity of me to be so cruel to you. You were a dependable and productive employee and I repaid you by hoping to send you to jail for my crimes. It's over for me. I can't control my cravings and desires. I don't care about my life. I am worthless. I ruined my life and the lives of those around me. I'm sorry you were in my path. I'm taking care of my problem. There will be no contending with a trial. I'm sorry for this mess, Phil.

I stared at the wall, numb. What was Hank's name doing in this note? Hank was involved in the robbery? Oh my God, I've been such a fool. Is that why Hank helped pin the robbery on Phil? Was it to avoid suspicion? How could

111

Hank throwaway his good life for more money? From the outside, it looked like he had plenty of money.

I walked over to the couch, fell into the cushions, slumped over and started crying.

It's over, this relationship must be over, I thought. *Damn, I liked the guy and loved the sex. How could I pick another loser? What is wrong with me? What about managing Hank's money for my new employer? How could I break up with him before I established a great client list at my new job? Would I lose this job if I didn't manage Hank's money – probably.*

Now I felt trapped. Shit, this is exactly what I didn't want to happen.

Wondering why Phil cared enough to send this note, I stared at the wall through tears. Was Phil was trying to blame Hank as his last despicable act? Was Phil doing what he always did – put the blame on someone else? He did understand his powerlessness over his relentless gambling desires before he died. Did he want to ruin Hank? Or did he want to make amends for his mistakes and come clean?

The questions were endless. Why send me a note, what about his wife? I certainly couldn't call Jenny and ask if she got an "I'm sorry" note. What if she didn't receive a note? I didn't want this note, that's for sure. It opened Pandora's Box with evil thoughts swimming in my head. Doubts about my relationship with Hank were swirling everywhere.

Still dazed, Hank called. I automatically answered – that was a big mistake.

"Hank, you're not going to believe this – I received Phil's apology note. I'm shocked."

"Are you okay? What did he say?"

"Yes, I'm surprised he confessed his sins, but I have to go. I'll call you later."

"Lauren, don't go. Please read the note to me. I want to hear what he wrote. I'm amazed Phil reached out to you. He made so many bad decisions when I was trying to help him. It was infuriating."

Why was Hank so concerned about Phil's note?

"Hank, I've got to go. I'll call you later, I need to think this situation through."

I hung up.

Hank called me right back. Regaining my composure, I didn't pick up. Hank's voice message had a fearful tone.

"Hey, I just wanted to let you know I love you and whatever Phil says, it is probably not true."

How could Hank be so concerned if he was innocent?

Do I show this letter to the authorities so they can arrest Hank? Did I really want Hank to be out of my life? I walked into my kitchen and poured a glass of red wine. I wanted to be numb to deal with this revelation. Madness was screaming in my head. I needed to sleep, and with any luck, receive guidance from the universe.

What would that guidance be?

Chapter 21

After a fitful night's sleep, I was grateful for the opportunity to go to work as I needed a major distraction. Hank was calling. I needed to talk with him but was sure he would persuade me that he was innocent to get out of being implicated in the robbery. It was time to put on my big girl pants and talk to him, but was I ready?

At work, I decided to read him the note and ask why his name was associated with the robbery. Just as I made up my mind to call Hank; he walked into my office.

"Nice digs you got here, Lauren," he said.

My heart started pounding, my cheeks flushed, "Thank you," was all I could say.

"You've been avoiding me, why?"

"Phil's note implicated you in the robbery. It said you were part of the robbery – that you and Phil would split the money."

"That's nonsense."

"Why would he lie? He was about to kill himself. He had nothing to protect. I'm not sure he knew we were a couple, but why mention you?"

"Phil was mad at me. He wanted to take me down because he knew my efforts got him captured. You know how crazy addicts are. They bite the hand that feeds them. He blamed me for his compulsive gambling and financial problems. If I was in the plan, why did he take the entire $22 million and I have nothing?"

"Good point, but maybe Phil double crossed you as well."

"Not so. I'm innocent. What do I need to do to prove it to you?"

"I don't know. I'm confused that's for sure. I really enjoyed our time together, but now I'm not sure. I can't understand why the note would mention you."

"I'm a victim, believe me. Phil's dying act was to complicate my life unnecessarily. He was jealous of me because I have money, a successful business and I'm single. Phil always talked about what a burden Jenny was and how lucky I was to be rid of that family."

"Hank, you know I want to believe you, but my head is swimming. Can I have a few days to think about this situation? I'm at a loss here."

"Okay, but I want to take you out to dinner tonight. We need to talk and I'm going back to Florida tomorrow."

"We do need to talk."

"Please ask any questions you want; I'm happy to answer them. I trusted Phil and, like you, I misplaced my trust. I'd like to get this problem resolved to your satisfaction. Get your questions and concerns together and let's talk tonight. Meet me at Gramercy Tavern at 7. Yes?"

"That's fine, but this situation is a mess."

"Agreed," Hank said sadly.

Chapter 22

Dinner with Hank was strained. While I wanted to believe him, I was filled with doubts and reservations. I couldn't understand why Phil would lie; he had nothing to lose. There was no need to put Hank's name in the note.

"Honey, you know Phil was an addict. He didn't take responsibility for his life."

"I believe that Hank, but he did apologize for setting me up as the fall guy for the robbery. He had some clarity before he killed himself; why mention you? The apology note was a surprise and why put your name in it?"

"He wanted to ruin me before he died," Hank continued. "I know this sounds self-centered, but I wonder if the only reason he wrote you the note was to destroy my great life. He was jealous of me, resented my help and was irate that I tracked his activities in Las Vegas which helped you. You said you weren't that close with him. Why send you this note? I believe his ulterior motive was to create problems for me. Why would I risk my good life for $11MM? I'm worth more than $11MM. The additional money would be nice, but I don't need to steal it. I make money the semi legal way, real estate development. I don't need to resort to bank robbery."

"That makes sense to me, let me think about your line of reasoning. By the way, this is as good a time as any to tell you that I go a 12-step meeting, Al-Anon. I go to a meeting generally once a week, read daily meditations and write about my challenges and joys. The meetings help me accept life as it is and not to resist the parts of life that I don't want. I want to grow spiritually and handle life with grace. I'm having difficulty rising above the mental chatter because of this situation."

"I hear great things about 12 step programs. I had a friend who felt everyone should incorporate the 12 steps into their life, whether they had an addiction or not."

"Sounds like good advice."

A smile came to my face, Hank was open and insightful. But I turned to him with a heavy heart.

"I am very concerned Phil mentioned you in the note. Was he really that resentful of you? Why would you turn to him for help processing the Sutton Place loan if you knew he was envious of you? Why were you so concerned about the contents of the note anyway?"

"I didn't realize the extent of his hatred of me until the note surfaced; then everything clicked. He wasn't responsive when I called him; he was reluctant to provide feedback on the loan process and he never thanked me for the cash flow that I was going to provide him. He argued with me every step of the way. The only reason I offered any help was to appease my ex, which I now regret."

"Yes, getting involved in other people's problems never works; no one wants help anyway; unless, of course, it's money. Then they want the money and to be left alone. You know the saying is: if you don't want to talk to someone, lend them money; then you'll never hear from them again."

"Amen sister." Hank continued about the program; it was an easier topic to discuss than the note.

"They say acceptance and gratitude are the keys to a happy life. Accepting life as it comes and being grateful for both the good and the bad makes life easier to enjoy. Forgiveness is another requirement for a happy life."

"Are you asking for forgiveness already?" I asked. "I still wonder as to why you underhandedly tried to get the second loan from Phil and not me? Why work with Phil who was a hot mess? I was your account manager and had the ability to get you the necessary money."

"Because Phil brought me the Sutton Place deal and said he would take care of everything; which included his controlling the loan process at the bank."

"This is not easy on me."

"I know, but it's not easy for me either."

"Okay, fair enough."

"So, to change the topic, how do you know more about 12 step programs then I do?" I asked.

"I've listened to my 12 step friends over the years. They are walking proof that people can change and live happier lives. I would say they are honorable, reliable folks. They live a life in service to others. It's not that the problems stop, it's how they handle the challenges. I paid attention because alcoholism runs in my family. Fortunately, it's not one of my addictions; but you are."

"Just happy we talked Hank. Your friendship changed my life. I hope I'm not making another mistake with my heart. I'm wary."

"I know. I'm concerned that Phil's one final act was throwing me under the bus. It's been a long time since I want someone the way I want you."

"That's nice to hear, but I need time."

"Okay," he said staring into my eyes. "I love you, Lauren. Let's go home. I'm not hungry."

"Me either."

The sadness was palatable at home. He kissed me gently and tenderly on the lips. We kissed for a long time; there was no urgency to this communication. His arms embraced me tightly; not letting go. His cock was hard, but he wasn't reaching for my privates. Hank pulled me on top of him as he laid on the couch. His arms engulfed me with his love.

"Lauren, I helped you solve the robbery and got you a job. I am here for you. We'll work together through life's ups and down. Kiss me darling."

The kiss was long with no space between us. His hands were on my head, caressing my hair.

He whispered, "I want this moment with you to last. Please don't give up on me."

His leg covered my ass as he nestled his foot between my legs. I was safe and warm.

Emotionally exhausted, I fell asleep on top of Hank. He didn't stir.

***

Two nights later with Hank back in Florida, he called me.

"Hi Hank. How are you? Thank you for the visit. I feel much better since we discussed Phil's note, but there are lingering thoughts of betrayal."

"Call me if you have specific questions; but meanwhile, where are your hands?"

"No place in particular, but I suspect your hand is on that oversized penis of yours."

"You know it."

"What are you doing to yourself?"

"I'm thinking of you, my dick is stiff and my hand is rubbing up and down my shaft. I hope your fingers are rubbing your clitoris by now."

"Yes, I'm wet just thinking about you. My fingers are circling my clit and I'm smearing the cream all over my kissing lips."

"Ahh, I wish your mouth was licking my penis and I was looking at the back of your head bouncing up and down."

"You mean as I rub my tongue on the underside of you shaft and cradle your balls in my hand?"

"Oh, God, what else would you do?"

I decided it was time to venture into unfamiliar sexual territory with this man.

"Put your whole cock in my mouth, open my throat and swallow you into me. I hope your hand is moving faster and spending an extra second rubbing the helmet of your penis. I'm taking your cock out of my mouth and rubbing my wet tongue down your shaft, licking your balls then putting one ball in my mouth at a time. I'm now spreading your legs apart and licking and pressing your taint. You swing your legs in the air and my tongue circles your ass. The wetness lubricates you and it's easy to insert a finger gently into your dark hole. You groan while your shaft pulsates with pleasure."

"Please don't stop talking, Lauren."

"My hands are squeezing your butt and your throbbing bone is in my mouth."

"What are you really doing?" Hank asked.

"I'm rubbing myself with my right hand and the left hand is playing with my nipple. I can smell your cock as it is going in and out of my mouth and see your erection grow. I'll be ready soon."

Even though Hank asked, it seemed that the momentum stopped when I mentioned me, so I went back to focusing on Hank.

"My mouth is back on your cock and I can feel the orgasm start from your anal cavity and course through your balls. Your machine is so rigid and red, when I rub my tongue around your rim, you stiffen."

"Your voice is making me stiffer; your breathing is in synch with me, you have to be ready, honey. I am about to explode," he said.

"Your juice shoots in the air hitting my face. I lick off the semen that is on your cock, kiss your stomach and then kiss your face. You lick the white juice off my face and thrust your tongue deep into my salty mouth."

"Ohhh."

Chapter 23

"Hi Greta, happy to see you at this meeting," I said.

"Hey, I have been running full steam to complete the proposal and open this business. I'm so excited, Lauren, but I haven't made time for the Al-Anon meetings. How are you?"

"I'm great, I think this program is starting to change my thought patterns. It turned out Phil killed himself in the holding cell."

"Oh, no. Are you okay?"

"At first, I felt terrible, but I quickly realized it was his doing, not mine. There was nothing I could do to save him. Even if he hadn't been caught, he would have tried to borrow more money after he bet and lost the $22 million dollars. The mob would have killed him eventually because he was gambling his life away. Thanks to this program, I know I couldn't help Phil; he didn't want my help anyway."

"Good point, Lauren."

"Hey, tell me about the proposal."

"Very well, I've been editing the document and working on finding a space. I'm looking at some buildings tomorrow. I'll keep you posted."

Chapter 24

"Lauren, please go to the Executive VP's office," my assistant, Joanna, said.

"Why? Do you know what he wants to talk about?" I asked.

"No."

After briefly reviewing my calendar to make sure I wouldn't miss any appointments, I put on a fresh smear of lipstick and hurried to my boss's office.

What could he possibly want? I've been working here for only four weeks, brought in $43 million dollars to manage, seems like I should *not* be called to the principal's office.

"Hi Lauren, please sit down."

"Thank you, Howard. Is there a problem?"

"No, no problem. I wanted to talk with you about the particulars of the robbery that your former boss committed. $22 million is a big number."

"Sure, I told your boss the story, but I'm happy to reiterate it for you."

"Thank you."

"Phil had me fill out paperwork for a second loan request for one of our customers and then he wanted me to give him the paperwork so he could process the documents. It was weird because I always completed and processed the paperwork."

"Oh, what happened next?"

"I'm not sure, Howard. Phil somehow got the escrow funds to be released without proper authorization and when the release paperwork did surface, it had my signature on it."

"I don't know if my former employer figured out how that step was completed, but Paul said that was my former employer's problem."

"Thank you for the information. Do you have any thoughts on how the money was released?"

"No, I don't. Why are you asking?"

"Oh, I just want to make sure we don't have any robberies like that at this bank; or if we do, it's me who gets away with $22 million."

I was not smiling. It was a creepy comment.

"There is a work party tonight. It'll be 6:30 PM at Pappardelle's on Columbus Ave, at 75th St. I hope you can attend. See you then?" Asked Howard.

"Sure, thanks for thinking of me."

I walked into Pappardelle's at 6:35 and saw Howard, but no one else from the bank. Howard was waiting at the bar.

"Where is everyone?" I asked.

"I wanted to be with just you. I didn't want other people distracting us."

"Howard, I'm dating someone else, but thank you for the compliment." I wanted to be rude, but as I report to

Howard, no sense losing my job in the first few weeks due to his stupidity and desires.

"Well, let's have dinner; we're here and the pasta is delicious."

I obliged him, fake smiling, fuming inside and making small, very small talk.

He kept at it; making clumsy comments about my looks and how good we'd be together.

"Lauren, I think about you all the time, how beautiful you are and wonder what you are doing on the lonely nights when your boyfriend isn't around."

I was repulsed.

"Lauren, I know you date Hank, but no one needs to know. We can have some fun together and be discreet about our relationship."

"What about your wife, Howard?"

"She doesn't need to know."

"I don't operate like that. I am a one-man woman."

"Oh, come on. You'll enjoy our time together. I'll make it worthwhile."

"No thank you, this conversation is making me uncomfortable. I want to be faithful to the man in my life, so please take my "no" as final. In addition, I don't think having a sexual relationship with my married boss is a good career move. I'm flattered, of course, but please let's discuss work and finish our meal."

"Okay, Lauren, but I can make your life easier."

"How?" I was sure to be disgusted again.

"I assign the accounts that come into our department from other bank divisions. I can send the more profitable accounts to you."

"Thank you, Howard, but I'm not interested in a sexual relationship with you. I hope you would be fair in doling out the accounts even if we are not in a sexual relationship."

"Oh, of course," he lied.

If I report this escapade to the bank, Howard and I both get fired – at best. At worst, I'm fired and Howard continues his predatory practices. If I keep this info to myself, Howard victimizes other women. What a choice.

Getting up from the table, I went to the ladies' room and turned on my cell phone voice recorder. I returned with a flushed face, but rage in check, so I thought.

"Howard, I hope you realize you put me in a very uncomfortable position. I respect you as my boss and a successful banker. I would expect the same courtesy from you."

"Of course, Lauren. I do respect you. I think we can have a productive working relationship."

"How is having sex together productive?"

"Not sex Lauren, you misunderstood me. I brought you out to dinner to see how I can help you be as successful as possible at the bank. If you need anything, please let me know."

He sat there with a shit-eating grin on his face. He's a serial sexual slayer. Women must have tried to record him when he was hitting on them and now, he is wise to the trick. Damn.

"Okay, Howard. Thank you for dinner and this chance to know you better. I look forward to working with you at the office."

I was humiliated but determined to catch this monster. *How?*

Chapter 25

The one nagging question that wouldn't go away: where was the last $4,150,000 that Phil didn't gamble away, but robbed from my former employer? The police must be looking for that money, but they didn't grill me on the whereabouts of the money once Phil was found. Did Phil tell them where the money is or does Hank have it? Is that why he stayed behind in Las Vegas?

Since the weekend was here and Hank was working; it was time to schedule Brett's services. I needed a massage to relieve stress; plus there were a few other benefits to this type of massage. I wondered if this was a betrayal to Hank but decided that there was no threat of a real relationship with Brett. Hank was protected. Was this a rationalization? How would I feel about Hank getting a happy ending with his massage? Is this living my life with integrity?

By 10:30 AM Saturday I was sitting on Brett's warm massage table.

"What type of massage do you want today?"

"I want a full-service massage," I answered. That seemed clear and discreet enough for me and Brett nodded his head in agreement with a small smile on his face as he walked out the door giving me privacy to undress.

After I took off my clothes and slipped between the soft sheets Brett knocked on the door and came in. The sound of his applying oil to hands and arms was intertwined with peaceful soft music filling the room.

"We'll start with your back. I'll try to release the stress."

I smiled, realizing how much has happened since Victor left and how far he was in my rearview mirror. While there were challenges with the divorce, I was grateful to have a job that I mostly enjoyed (except for Howard), a caring boyfriend (who hopefully wasn't a bank robber); and I had a new friend in Greta.

Brett rubbed each side of my neck with his fingers while his thumbs massaged the spine in the back of the neck. He gently pulled my head toward him to lengthen my spine. He walked over to my side and repeatedly pressed down on my shoulder and the opposite hip with his palms, elongating and energizing my back. He worked on the other side as well.

Then a long, luxurious stroke starting from the top of my shoulders with his thumbs stimulating each side of my spine and his fingers extending outward. As his hands went down my back, he lowered his elbows, so his entire forearm was pressing on my back. His hands moved to the sides of my body and up to my shoulders. His fingers delayed a few seconds on the sides of my breasts that were squished outward. His hands went into my armpits, up to the shoulder blades and massaged the top of my shoulders. He repeated the stroke many times elongating my back each time. It was a long, loving stroke that touched areas that were rarely addressed.

His total attention was on me. He found a knot and toggled the stress with lots of pressure, it was uncomfortable for a moment, but the knot disappeared as quickly as it was found.

As Brett moved his hands and arms down my back, his body weight squeezed out stress with my shoulders giving way to his body dominating me. I could feel his breath on my back as he leaned forward moving his hands to my glutes. His nails dug into my ass just before he swept his hands around the curve of my butt. He pressed hard on both sides of my hips and then spread his hands on my glutes squeezing and releasing those muscles. Love juice dripped out of my pussy.

The repeated slow stroke down my back with the full force of Brett's testosterone on me caused heart palpitations. With his hands on my ass, followed by massaging upper and inner thighs, my pussy started panting. I fantasized about rolling over, spreading my legs and pulling him on top of me, but I didn't do it.

He moved down the table, his hands on either side of my upper thigh and massaged slowly down my leg. His fingers used a circular motion on each side of the leg with his thumbs pressing hard on my femoral shaft. Every six inches or so, Brett moved back up the thigh to touch the sensitive inside thigh skin. After lightly massaging that area for a few minutes he started back down the leg in a relaxed manner. I was not relaxed, breathing heavier, heart pounding with a longing screaming out from between my legs.

He circled my knee area, tickling the back, then slowly moving up the leg. He repeatedly returned to my groin area causing me to squirm. Could he smell my affections? He seemed oblivious as he massaged the calf with intermittent visits to the upper thigh. Thoroughly aroused, I needed to come.

"I remember you like your feet massaged, right?" Brett said.

"Yes," was all I could say.

He twisted the toe part of the foot inward and the arch outward. He rubbed between the toes and pulled on them. My sexual desire lessened and I started to relax. Brett became aware that I was not tantalized. He finished the feet, washed his hands and slowly went back up the leg. He repeated this teasing process on the other leg and said, "Please flip over."

As I rolled onto my back, I felt the wet spot on the sheet. I wasn't embarrassed but wondered how long I could hold on.

Brett massaged my head with fingers pressing on my scalp and the hair not getting tangled in his fingers. He rubbed my forehead and put pressure on my temples followed by circular motions on the temples. His fingers moved down to the jaw located by the ears. Pressing hard he released stress from that area.

He spread his fingers wide as he gently moved down the neck to my nipples. He squeezed my breasts on his way down to my hips. His hands moved to the side of the body, over the rib cage and back to my breasts. He played with my bosoms for a long time, alternating between gently rubbing oil on them, pinching the nipples and pulling on them. He squeezed them together and added more oil to my mountain of mammaries. I fantasized about his penis placed in the valley but tried to stay focused on my sensations.

The stomach was well oiled and his figure eight motion between my chest and stomach became intoxicating. My chest heaving, pussy throbbing – again.

He moved down to my hips and slipped his hands between my legs. I knew he felt the heat and wetness.

He whispered, "Do you want me to touch you?"

"Yes."

He put his entire hand over my crack and gently pushed against me. Two fingers slipped in, then moved up to my clitoris and started circling my labia. The first crest of joy came over me as he made direct contact with my nerve center, but the pleasure didn't stop there.

For the first time, he leaned down and bit my nipple while he circled my most private parts. My back arched and he whispered, "Cum for me, baby."

A pulsating energy started from my vagina and vibrated to every part of my body, sending a smile to my lips, deepening of my breath and a tightening of my muscles.

Brett moved his hands to my inner thighs, down the leg to the knee, then back to my hips. He leisurely circled from one hipbone to the other with a dip in the middle to stimulate me. His hands were everywhere; I couldn't keep track of his fingers. I only knew I was engulfed in a sea of pleasure with joy swirling around the room.

I couldn't stop the sensations and didn't want to. Eyes closed, out of breath, my body demanded I stay on the roll. Warm sensations started between my hips and grew stronger with every stroke. My eyes rolled back, toes curled and stomach sweating as Brett caressed my tits, rubbed my clit, and licked my neck. Back arching, moaning with white space surrounding me, my body disappearing with only joy and love surrounding me.

Sometime later, drained, with my stomach heaving, trying to catch a breath, Brett smiled and leaned down.

"Don't you want the grand finale?"

I was interested, but not if Hank and I were a couple. I wanted Hank to be the only man inside me.

Would Brett ever be inside of me? Should I see Brett while I'm with Hank?

Chapter 26

Back to the $4,150,000 question: where is that money?
Obsessing, I wanted to help Greta open the women's center
and to verify that Hank was clean, once and for all. Phil
knew, but he was dead. What did Hank know? I wondered.
Perhaps the money was still at the casino. Would the casino
manager help Hank get the funds? Probably not; he'd keep
the money for the casino or, more likely, himself.

Enough pondering, I'll ask Hank about the last of the
$22 million. No, maybe not. He already denied knowing
about the robbery, but the direct approach has always been
my style.

Hank picked up the phone on the first ring.

"Hi Hank," I said.

"Lauren, so great to hear from you."

"Thanks, I'm glad we are okay."

"How are you, honey?"

"I'm good, but I have a question for you."

"Shoot."

"Where do you think remaining $4,150,000 is?"

"I don't know," was the nervous reply.

"Really, do you think your friend at the Palazzo knows? I suspect the funds are hidden at the casino. Didn't you say you had some business with John when I left Las Vegas?"

"Yes, but it wasn't about the stolen funds. Why are you asking?"

"I just learned that the Feds have not found the money and I need funds to help Greta open up a center for abused women."

"That sounds noble, but you have a full-time job, how are you going run two businesses?"

"I'm running my banking business; Greta will run the women's shelter. It's time to help women. Banks don't provide loans to women with the same frequency as they do men. Women need better access to capital – especially when the business is geared to helping women."

"When did you become so philanthropic?"

"It started when I met Greta at Al-Anon. She wants to open a facility to provide battered women and their children with a safe haven."

"I didn't know about this vision; why didn't you share your plan with me?"

"Hank, it takes time to learn about someone's life. Besides, I am sharing with you now – don't you want a little Lauren mystery?"

"No, I'd like to know everything about you. You are mystery enough. If you believe in her, I'd like to learn more about this operation. You'll probably have to fund her operation forever, not just upfront funds; because that type of operation doesn't typically sustain itself."

"She's working on getting grants to create a center and start the operation. She's planning on establishing relationships with government agencies that will provide clients and pay for her services. If she can keep her costs low, she might be able to turn a small profit."

"Perhaps we can help her. How much money does she need to start the operation and how much will it cost to keep the center open?"

"I'll check, but does this mean you'll help her?"

"It's a firm maybe."

"Okay, I'll get the numbers to you, thanks Hank. I want to help other women organizations as well. Do you think we can access the last $4,150,000?"

"You are persistent," Hank stammered, "but John, the casino manager isn't going to share his windfall with us. He might have the money, but I'm surprised if the feds didn't successfully shake him down for the money. I guess Phil was shrewd enough to throw away the casino receipts outlining the cash he deposited at the casino before he was arrested."

"I have to go to Las Vegas in a few days anyway, I'll visit John and see his reaction when I mention the cash. When I come back, why don't you come down for the weekend?"

"Sounds great."

Chapter 27

Greta called. "Hey, can you meet me? I found a perfect building in Harlem."

"Really, what's the deal?" I asked.

"The owner wants to sell the place for $125,000. The place is perfect, it is an abandoned hotel. There are living quarters for ten families upstairs, two large meeting rooms and a kitchen on the first floor and several offices."

"That sounds like what you need."

"Yes, but I'm nervous about any mechanical, water or electrical defects in the building. According to the realtor, the bones to the building are strong, so at least I don't have to worry about the building collapsing."

"That's promising, when are you having an inspector look at the place?" I asked.

"Tomorrow."

"You are on it! Do you have the finished business proposal?"

"Yes, I just need pricing to renovate the building. Let's meet tomorrow for dinner."

"Great, how about Little Luzzo's on 96th Street?"

"Sure, 7 PM?"

"Great, bring the updated draft of the proposal."

Greta was at the restaurant when I arrived. She looked apprehensive.

Pizza and focaccia bread sandwiches were the specialties of this favorite local brownstone pizzeria, so what could be wrong?

"Want to order a meatball and onion pizza?" I asked.

"Sure. Here's the new proposal with actual numbers based on renovating the building and the money from the foundations I've contacted so far."

"Nice. Did you found out how hard it is to establish a relationship with government agencies that help battered women, and more importantly how much they pay you for your services?"

"Yes, I must complete a ridiculous amount of paperwork and pass an on-site inspection, but as long as I have what they require, I should be okay. They pay between $2,400 to $3,600 every month for counseling services, room and board."

"That's good news."

"I believe I can get $300,000 in grants – if all goes well. The problem is that the money will come in sporadically and only once the building is renovated, open and operational."

"How much money do you need?"

"It's a rough number, but I'll need $125,000 to purchase the building."

"Or you could take out a mortgage."

"Yes, but I'm not sure I'll get a mortgage, my finances are in sad shape. The contractor said it will take $150,000 to get the building up to code and build it out according to my requirements. The realtor was right, apparently the bones, water and electrical systems are in good shape."

"Don't forget to have the lot evaluated for environmental contamination. Hotels aren't typically polluters, but you have to check."

"Okay, I'll look into an environmental analysis."

"Hey, what are you going to name your organization?"

"I don't know. What do you think about Safe Haven?"

"I like it, but the name pertains to protection only. You might want to offer other services to women and the name limits that activity."

"Good point. What do you recommend?"

"That's tough, let me think. How about Wonder Women Services or Greta's Grotto?"

"Very funny. How about Women for Women? Would the acronym of WFW work?"

"Not a fan of acronyms, but I like Women for Women. Does that mean that men can't work in the organization? Is that limiting?"

"Damn, this is annoying. How about Strive to Thrive?"

"It's close. How about Women's Hope? Or Center of Caring?"

"That's it: Center of Caring and Hope. I like all that the name implies: a place of caring and hope. Thanks, Lauren."

"Great, give me a few days to review the proposal. It will take me a minute to review the numbers."

"No problem and thanks."

Chapter 28

Walking into Hank's apartment, I felt rejuvenated between an easy flight, cab ride and expectations of Hank's hands all over me, but I was to be disappointed.

The apartment looked out over palm trees circling a bright blue pool. Big orange birds of paradise, pink Mexican petunias and zinnias popped out in clusters of cheery colors. Hank's place had a white leather couch, surrounded by two glass end tables with a cooper coffee table in the middle. On the opposite wall there was a mega sized TV screen. To the left was a kitchen with windows overlooking the beautiful landscape. The cabinets were pickled oak with dark soap stone countertops. The middle island provided lots of cabinet space, but I wondered how many women sat on the island with Hank between their legs.

What is wrong with me? Why is my mind going to jealousy? Hank has been very devoted to me, but there was a nagging about his involvement in the robbery. If he was a thief, what else was he capable of doing?

Hank emerged from the bathroom and walked right over to me; put his arms around me and said, "We are going to do something different today."

I gulped.

"What?" I asked.

"I'm entering you from the rear."

Not a fan of anal, my face went deadpan. I should have known it was coming, I did mention inserting my finger in his hole during phone sex. Damn, what was I thinking?

"You don't like anal, my dear?"

"Not really, I've never had an orgasm that way."

"Well, today is your lucky day. I'll make sure you have several orgasms before, during and after I enter you."

He led me to his massive bedroom with a king size bed covered by a matte black quilt with six checkered black and white pillows propped up against a black tufted headboard. The bench at the end of the bed had black teddy, a single red rose, and a vibrator – an Eroscillator.

I had my first orgasm with a vibrator in college. Within a week of the vibrator's arrival, most of the girls on our dormitory floor bought their own nob-pleasing vibrator; that's where I discovered the importance of the clitoris in an orgasm. There are other body parts that heighten pleasure (the brain for one), but the clitoris has always been my go-to-spot for memorable explosions.

Once I learned the value of the stimulating the nob, sex became much more interesting to me. For me, the walls of the vagina didn't produce nearly as intense an orgasm as the clitoris, but as every woman knows, there are many things and ways that bring a woman to orgasm – it all depends. That's why there is no Viagra for women; it's not just a physical issue – there are many variables that lead to the female release; physically, emotionally and mentally.

Hank put his hand on my ass and guided me to the bed. He started kissing my neck and breathing deeper. I didn't like where this session was headed, but hopefully Hank was different than Victor. Victor liked anal since it was his first sexual experience, but like the rest of his sexual repertoire, I didn't orgasm. Why stay with him? I wanted to blame myself, but instead kept my mind on the task at hand. No sense living in the unchangeable past.

Hank walked over to the nightstand, opened the drawer and pulled out rosemary scented massage oil. I tried to distract him, but he was not to be stopped. Putting his hand in my pants, between my legs, he started rubbing my hot button which felt good, but I was apprehensive. His mouth covered my lips and his tongue slid into me. His intensity was overpowering me. He unbuttoned my shirt and pants. As the top came off, the bra followed immediately. I was wet. Pushing me onto the bed, pulling the pants off, he started licking me. Maybe this session won't be yucky after all. He licked my inner thighs with a slow, warm, wet stroke. My pussy oozing love juice.

He reached over to the dark and light wood art deco nightstand and picked up the bottle of oil, squirted oil on his hands and started rubbing my hips. He immediately flipped me over and put his large oiled hands on my ass, digging down into my muscles. The response from my muscles was to tighten.

"Relax honey, nothing's going to happen without you wanting it."

"Then I don't think you'll be having anal today," I responded.

"Don't be too sure, I just started the love making. We have many cells to stimulate before we get to your bottom."

Interesting, I thought.

As his warm hands kneaded my ass, my muscles relaxed. He started kissing and licking my lower back.

"Lauren, I can't stop thinking about you. You are my world."

"Wow, you must really want anal, Hank," I teased.

"I want all of you."

Was he flattering me to get his way? Probably.

Hank's circles on my ass were getting smaller as they revolved around my anus. He poured more oil on his hands and started gently pushing down between my cheeks. His other hand was rubbing my nob and slipping into my vagina to keep the juices flowing. And they were flowing.

His finger slid into my anus; I was excited. It felt different, but not sexual. I prefer other orifices penetrated. With his hot breath and tongue on my back, the walls of my box quivered. I started gasping for air.

"Not yet," he said. "I've got to be inside of you."

He inserted two fingers as he circled around the walls of my anus, stretching out my sphincter. It was distracting, but he went back to caressing the clitoris with his other hand. Was this a pleasant sensation?

Hank spread my legs wide on the bed and positioned himself between my legs. He took his fingers out of my rear, leaned over and said, "it is time for your first climax."

First, he entered my pussy, shoving his throbbing member in as hard as he could. I didn't like the roughness, the crudeness of the act.

"Clamp down on me," he demanded.

I submitted.

"Do it again, and again."

The rhythm, the squeezing and the pounding started a sensation of pleasure that I couldn't stop. He smacked my ass and said, "Keep moving those hips, don't stop."

Hank didn't stop. After my first mini eruption, he put his fingers back in my dark hole, pulled out his cock from my pussy, squirted oil on it and pressed the tip of his shaft directly on top of my hole as he pulled his fingers out. The penis slowly penetrated those tight muscles. Hank let out a guttural sound of desire.

He slowly inserted his meat inside me. After entering me for a several inches, he withdrew his member an inch or two; followed by a deeper insertion. He didn't stop rubbing my slit and demanded that I tighten my pussy and sphincter at the same time. It woke up all the nerve endings in my undercarriage.

His left hand rubbed my clit, his right hand squeezed my ass as he rhythmically entered and withdrew himself with increasing speed. His breathing and grunts got louder. I felt beads of sweat fall on my back from Hank as he was losing his composure.

"I can feel you tightening everything inside; it is going to make me cum very soon."

"Me too," was all I could say as I lost track of where I was. The only sensation I felt was the erect penis stiffening followed by a warm, wet sensation.

After kissing my back, Hank excused himself and headed to the bathroom for clean-up. I wasn't going to put my lips on his large extremity for at least another two showers, but that orgasm was different. I couldn't move my body. I certainly felt the expansion of my sphincter but appreciated the waves of elation as they rolled through my body.

I must have drifted to another place because when I woke, Hank was fully clothed and standing in front of his closet safe. I didn't know he had a safe. He was turning the dial when I heard a loud click, signifying that the safe was open.

He checked over his shoulder and said, "Recover from the anal, honey?"

"Yes, thank you," I said with my eyes still closed.

"Just getting some documents for a contractor."

Opening my eyes, I saw seven stacks of money and Hank's back. The stacks of money were about 15 inches tall, and one stack was about half the height of the other six. *Big safe with lots of green,* I thought. It certainly appeared to be more than emergency money.

Was it Hank's share of the leftover funds from the robbery?

"Hank, how did your conversation with John go?"

"I asked him about the last $4MM that Phil didn't spend, but he denied having access to the funds. I believe him."

"Why do you have so much cash in you safe?"

"It is not the $4 million, Lauren. Occasionally, a customer pays cash for part of a project. I oblige them by lowering my rates and using the cash for spending money. I don't go ATMs very often. You still suspicious of me?"

"No, not really. Just surprised to see so much cash."

Was he a bank robber? Why won't this apprehension go away?

Chapter 29

I couldn't forget the image of the money during the flight home. Why was I so obsessed with his cash? It's not mine.

What was the total value of all those bills? I saw a hundred number on some of the bills. Were they all hundreds? Wow, that is serious cash. I knew $100,000 equals 4.3 inches of $100-dollar bills, so each 15-inch piles equals about $350,000. Was there almost $2.5MM in the safe? That is more than walking around money. Did Hank split the funds with John in Las Vegas?

What was my plan, anyway, swindle the money from Hank? Be like Phil. Is that who I've become? Even to help establish a women's center, to steal wasn't me or *was it*? I didn't like the prospect of prison the first time and certainly didn't want to go to jail because of my own greed or desire to help. I respected myself enough not to steal – at least I thought so.

I needed to go to an Al-Anon meeting. I wasn't thinking clearly. Thankfully, the message was about doing the next right thing. Seemed like a topic I needed to review. Even though Phil stole money and lost his integrity; I didn't need to go down that path. But I was fantasizing about the money and justifying the impure thoughts to help build a women's center. It was destructive thinking and those thoughts did me no good. I started reviewing my gratitudes: job, Hank/sex, health, friends and life.

Fortunately, Greta was at the meeting. We went to dinner after the gathering. I wasn't very hungry, so I had a cup of herbal tea, but Greta was ravenous and ordered a turkey club with French fries and a chocolate milkshake.

She was excited about the women's home and had accomplished lots since we last talked. She discussed her vision and the costs with the contractor. She determined the startup costs and the number of employees and clients needed to support the center. In addition, she had received her 501©3 designation, which meant she was a legal charity. Because of her volunteer work, she had made contacts in the field; knew where she could purchase slightly used furniture and had a few social workers that wanted to work with her. She had the environmental report completed; the tests were negative. The closing contracts weren't signed because she needed cash to purchase the building, but the seller and the contractor were ready to go once the cash was available. The only thing missing was cash.

Hank offered to help; it was time to approach him. I called him once I got home.

"Hey Hank, how are you?"

"Great to hear from you honey. How was your day? I missed you the moment you left."

"Thanks, Hank. I miss you too. I called to discuss the women's safe house."

"Not to talk dirty to me? I'm hurt."

I smiled.

"Greta found a place in Harlem. She has: a good business plan with realistic numbers, her charity certification, a good environmental report and now, just needs money."

"Oh, is that all she needs? How much?"

"She can buy the building for $125,000 and renovate it for about $150,000. Her startup costs will be $35,000 and she'll need about $25,000 to pay the workers during the lean first few months."

"That's $335,000! That's a chunk of money."

"She thinks she can get grants possibly up to $300,000, but she can't count on that money until she is reviewed and approved by the foundations. She has to be up and running for the foundations to take interest in her shelter."

"So, what do you want to do?"

"I know you've already done tons for me, but I'd like to be able to provide her with the cash she needs to buy and renovate the building that's $265,000. Plus a little more if things go sideways."

"How sideways?"

"Up to 25%?" I suggested.

"That's over $66,000 sideways. I'd call that a sideswipe, not sideways."

"Yeah, I hear you, but she won't get any funds until she's up and running, and I believe she is capable of running this project and it is a great cause. What do you think?"

"Aside from the headache I'm getting, I wish you could be with me tonight."

"Thanks, Hank, what do you think about this project?"

"What are you wearing?"

"Can we stay on point until this financial conversation is over?"

"Okay, but now that I hear the high costs of this project, I'm getting less interested."

"Really?" I asked.

"Yes, I thought you were talking about $25,000 to $50,000. Over $300,000 is way more than I wanted to contribute to a nonprofit."

"I'm sorry to hear that, Hank."

"Sweetie, look, I'll contribute some funds, but hundreds of thousands are too big a commitment on my part."

"How did you ever determine the funds required to purchase a building, renovate it and start a business would be in the $25,000 to $50,000 range?" I asked.

"I didn't reason it through. I wanted the number to be less than $50,000 and that's where I stopped thinking."

"Look, we can't buy, build and open the Center of Caring and Hope without your funds, Hank."

"Damn it, Lauren, I can't provide the funding you need."

"Yes, you can Hank. You don't have any major projects right now that require money and you have a boatload of green in your safe."

"That's my cash to spend the way I want."

"That's true, possession is 90% of the law."

"What's that mean?"

"Proving the money resulted from your projects and not from the $4,150,000 left over from Phil's robbery may be difficult. That cash in combination with Phil's letter to me might cause some concern by the authorities."

"What the hell, Lauren. I get the evidence needed to exonerate you and you blackmail me?"

"Sounds harsh, when you say it like that. But the question is: were you involved in putting me in that spotlight?"

"God, NO, Lauren. And I don't have the unspent cash from the robbery either."

"Sorry to hear that Hank. If you did, perhaps it would be easier for you to provide me with $325,000."

"It's not easy, but you can have the cash, if I get Phil's letter from you."

"Want to get rid of the evidence Hank?"

"I don't want you blackmailing every time you need cash."

"Fair enough. How do you want to handle the transaction?"

Chapter 30

It was time to talk with Paul Tannery, the head of my department, about how the accounts were doled out. I wasn't sure protocol was to make an appointment with Paul or just walk in. I walked by his office to see if he was busy. He wasn't.

"Hi Paul, how are you?"

"Good, Lauren. It's great to see you. You've been doing a fantastic job bringing in assets. Thank you for your hard and diligent work. What can I do for you?"

I smiled but cringed inside wondering how long Hank's account would be under my management.

"I understand that this organization gets referrals from other departments and I wondered how you decided who the account manager should be."

"Yes, I typically give that responsibility to Howard. Is there a reason you are asking?"

"Yes, I wondered how Howard makes that decision."

"My understanding is that he rotates the handouts with his team as each account comes into his office. Is there a problem?"

"No, I just wanted to make sure favoritism wasn't involved. Thanks for your time, Paul. I really enjoy working here."

As I walked out of his office, I saw Brenda, one of my coworkers, flying out of Howard's office, visibly upset.

I didn't know Brenda but felt I should show some compassion. I followed her into the ladies' room. She was standing at the sink with her head down, tears dripping.

"Hi Brenda. Is there anything I can do to help?"

"No, no one can help me. I've been having a rough time here at work, my account base is light, and Howard keeps putting pressure on me to bring in more money to manage."

"Oh, I'm so sorry to hear that. Is that all Howard is asking from you?"

"Why do you ask?"

"I don't know, Howard has a lot of interests."

"Yes," Brenda said, "he harassed me for sex. It's been six months of his nagging, I'm sick of it."

"Sorry, he's been trying to get into my pants too. It's disgusting."

"The problem is that I don't have any evidence. I've tried to record him a few times, but he seems to have a six sense and clams up."

"Maybe we could put a recorder in his office. What do you think? It's probably illegal," I suggested.

"I don't want to get in trouble with the law."

"I hear you. I don't want to worry about jail time either," I said.

"There must be something we can do."

"I don't want to go to Paul Tannery, do you?"

"No, but there must be a way. I think I'll do a Google search on our friend Howard and see if he has a police record. I have a friend who's a policeman," Brenda said.

"Sounds like a great idea, I'll do some research on our friend as well."

***

After going back to my office and spending a half an hour googling Howard I noticed he switched jobs frequently. More importantly, he worked at my former employer's but left before I arrived. Interesting, I never heard his name. I wondered if he was fired because of sexual allegations. I knew the woman in human resources. Was I close enough to her to make this call?

"Hi Lorraine, Lauren here."

"Hey Lauren, I hear you got a sweet deal. Congratulations. Are you happy at City?"

"Yes, thank you. I have an odd request for you. I report to a man named Howard Glub. I understand he used to work at your place, but left after only a year and a half of service."

"Lauren, I can't really talk about Howard's case."

"I understand Lorraine, but Howard has been sexually harassing at least two women in this office. When they try to record him, he seems to know and behaves accordingly. Do you have any suggestions for resolving this challenge?"

"So sorry, Lauren. I can't give you the details about Howard, but Howard has some criminal cases in the system. I believe this is public knowledge."

"How did you get him out of your office?"

"One of the ladies here recorded him; that's probably why he's wise about being recorded again. But we did not press charges; we didn't want the publicity. He was asked to resign."

"Thanks, Lorraine. I really appreciate your honesty. I will keep you as the source between the two of us."

I marched into Brenda's office and said, "Howard has a record of sexual misconduct. Contact your police officer and see what information you can get. There's got to be other ways to prove his guilt. Ask your police officer for suggestions."

Brenda picked up the phone before I left her office.

"Close the door, Lauren, I don't want Howard hearing this conversation."

"Okay, do you want me to stay for this conversation?"

"Yes."

"Hi Sean, it's Brenda. Yes, everything is fine, thanks for asking. Things good with you? Great, I have a question about handling sexual harassment at the workplace."

I couldn't hear what Sean was saying, but it seemed he was concerned.

"No, everything is fine, but we have a man named Howard Glub in our office who has been propositioning his female employees for sex. We know of two instances but suspect there are more."

"We want to put a recording device in his office, but is that illegal?"

"Yes, I see."

Brenda looked up at me and shook her head, inferring that it is illegal to put a recording device in someone's office without their knowledge.

"Oh, I see, we should document every instance where he approaches us. Write down the date, time, place and words he uses, how he handles himself, and how he made us feel. Okay got it."

"Can you look up his name and see if he has any record or judgments against him?"

"Uh huh," after a few minutes Brenda said, "he has several sexual misconduct cases brought against him, but they were settled out of court."

"Okay Sean, this is very helpful. Thank you so much. Please send me any details you can and we'll talk soon."

Brenda looked up at me. "So, Howard is a serial sexual predator and has had a few cases filed against him but they were all settled out of court. Interesting. I wonder how much money he paid."

"So we have to document every sexual advance from him, correct?" I asked.

"Yes. I don't think we should go to Paul with this information yet, do you?"

"No, I don't," I said. "We need hard evidence to support our accusations."

I went back to my office and typed what happened at the dinner with Howard. Between Hank and this record keeping am I setting myself up for another firing?

Chapter 31

Hank flew up to New York City the following week. He was to be in town for four days, but he wasn't staying at my place. I wondered if he wanted to discuss the cash and letter transfer and if that was the reason he wasn't staying with me. Was I doing the right thing by blackmailing him for the funds or was I being short sighted? I wasn't sure he was innocent in the robbery, but is that any reason to take $325,000 from him, even though the money is going for a good cause?

Hank charged into my office at 6 PM after a day full of meetings in the city.

My cheeks flushed and mouth open I said, "Hi Hank."

"How are you? You hungry?" he asked.

I stood up and walked over to Hank.

"I'm surprised to see you, Hank. Why are you here?"

Howard walked by my office and saw Hank. He came in and introduced himself; it was awkward.

"Nice to meet Lauren's boss," said Hank.

"Thank you," said Howard, "it's so very nice to meet you."

Hank smiled and asked about how Howard's responsibilities. Howard was sufficiently vague and elusive; I could tell Hank was not impressed.

After what seemed to be in interminably long time, Howard finally excused himself to leave.

Hank turned to me and said, "Is that guy always creepy?"

"Yes," I said.

"Oh, how so?"

"Nothing significant, I don't interact with him that much."

"Why do I get the feeling you are evading me?"

"I'm not, Hank, are you sure you want to have dinner with me?"

"Yes, we need to discuss our business transaction. I'll be moving my assets eventually, but for now I'm keeping them under your management. It's too much work to transfer the assets so soon after they were delivered here. I expect you to be smart about my investments and run any trades by me before you execute them."

"Fair enough, Hank. Thank you."

"Let's swing by Paul's office to say hello. I want to thank him for the way he handled your transition and wish him continued success here at the bank," Hank continued.

Embarrassed by all that Hank had done for me and how I showed my appreciation by blackmailing him; I looked down at the carpet.

Sure enough Paul was in his office.

"Hi Paul," Hank said.

"Hey Hank, great to see you," Paul said as he rose from his desk. "Thank you for sending Lauren to us. She is our top producer this month. She fits right in with our team."

"That's great. How does Howard fit in?"

Damn, Hank smelled a problem and now he is chasing down the scent. I hope this conversation doesn't pique Paul's curiosity.

"Oh," Paul said, "he oversees our eight account managers, including Lauren. He's been at the bank for seven months. Did you meet him?"

"Yes, how did he come by way of City?"

"He was recommended by one of our board members. Is there a reason you are asking?"

"No, seems like a decent guy."

I knew that was not what Hank was thinking, but it seemed to satisfy Paul's questions.

I was wary, what was Hank up to? How could he know about Howard so quickly?

***

"Lauren, we must have a very private conversation. Can we order Chinese and eat at your apartment? I'll leave once we finish our conversation and dinner."

He smiled.

"No problem, Hank. I appreciate your patience. And I'm sorry. You've shown me much kindness, and I'm blackmailing you. I hope most of the funds will be returned to you, but I can't guarantee it. It's the very thing Phil did which I hated."

"Damn it, I'm innocent. And now your greed ruined the best relationship I ever had."

"Sorry," was all I could say.

What was I doing?

Chapter 32

Brenda looked upset as I walked past her office.

"You okay?" I asked.

"No, Howard fired me today."

"Really, the guy is a sexual predator and he has the audacity to fire you? What are you going to do?"

"I don't know just yet. I'm thinking about my options, but I don't want to cause trouble for the bank. I have an illogical sense of loyalty to this organization."

"I hear you, but it will be a problem for the bank sooner or later. They've got to learn about Howard. I don't really want to, but if you need me, I'll come forward with our interaction. The problem is it was only one time. You need more validations of your experience."

"Yes, you're right. I asked two other women if they had problems with Howard and they both looked as if they had seen a ghost and clammed up."

"That's not good," I said. "Guess everyone wants to keep their jobs."

"Yeah, I'm talking to an attorney tonight. I'll let you know the strategy when it is developed. Thanks for your support, Lauren."

"What's your personal cell Brenda?"

"Good idea, 917 438 6683. What's your number?" Brenda asked.

"917 232 3889. Call any time."

"Thanks."

As I walked into my office, Howard was right on my tail.

I turned and said, "Good morning Howard. Is there something on your mind?"

"Yes," he responded, looking glum.

"I had to fire Brenda. She wasn't pulling in the numbers we need."

"Oh, I'm sorry to hear that, I liked Brenda. Did Paul approve of the firing?"

"It was my decision. I'm responsible for the numbers and we need producers. Do you know of any other talent that has a client base like yours?"

"No, I don't Howard."

"Too bad, I need another hitter. Meet me for lunch, we need to talk about account managers."

"I can't, Howard, I have lunch with a client," I lied.

"Oh, too bad, drinks then."

"I can't, Howard. Look, I respect your business acumen, but I felt uncomfortable at our last dinner and I don't want to cross over any work boundaries. I like this job and want to keep things professional."

Howard glared at me; his ears flushed.

"I'm sorry Howard. You are an interesting man, but I'm involved with Hank and that's as complicated as I want my life to be."

"Oh, no problem Lauren, I'm sorry to hear this, but I understand," Howard lied.

The insincere speech and smirk of a fake smile was unnerving.

I sat down at my desk and opened email. It was time to work and put the ugliness of last night and the morning behind me. I recorded Howard's invitation. He was disturbing, spine chilling.

As the day went on, the horror of the morning faded. Making calls, strategizing on investments and executing trades helped me get into my work rhythm. In the afternoon, I made a few cold calls for new clients and caught up on market research. I felt safe in my office; I had the power to say "No" to Howard there. By the time I went home, Howard's office was dark, very dark.

Once I got home, I called Hank to follow up on last night's conversation. I needed to see how he was going to transfer the funds to me. He was home and happy to talk.

"Hey Hank, I need Greta to open a checking account for her Center for Caring and Hope. That is the account where we should deposit the funds, don't you think?" I asked.

"Sure, I've been giving it some thought. I know you were talking about giving her the funds directly, but I am a developer and could contribute in a meaningful way. What I'd like to do is purchase the building and act as the general contractor over the project. This way I can manage the costs and complete the project on time and on budget."

"So you would own everything?" I snapped.

"Well, only during the purchase and renovation phase. We can draw up a contract that guarantees Greta owns the building within a year, no matter how far along the project is. If there are problems, or if things go well, Greta has the building."

"Hank, that sounds fair. Thank you for keeping a level head in the middle of this robbery."

"Stop it, Lauren. Yes, I'm disappointed by the way you handled this financing and it permanently changed our relationship, but you don't owe me any favors."

Was that guilt on Hank's part? I wondered if that meant Hank was involved in the robbery. *Could it be?*

***

The next morning, I called Greta with the good and the bad news. We had funding, but I used blackmail to get it – not my finest hour.

"Greta?"

"Hey Lauren, how are you?"

"You are not going to believe this news. I have the funding you need. You'll have to give up ownership of the building for the first year, but you'll own the place soon enough."

"How's that?"

"Hank will buy the building and have it renovated to your specifications. He is real estate developer and has the skills to handle this type project. After the project is complete, he will transfer the building to you, free of charge. We're both hoping some of the foundation funding will be used to pay Hank back. I didn't treat Hank well, after all he's done for me and I feel shitty about the blackmail. But he has the skills, money and know how, so he should manage the renovations of the building until it is complete."

"Shit, Lauren, I didn't want to compromise your integrity to get the funding for this project."

"I know, it was my decision. Before I got married, I blew up intimate relationships frequently. I clearly went back to that bad habit. I still wonder if Hank was involved in shady business dealings with Phil. I have to admit that I used that scenario as an excuse for my bad behavior."

"Lauren, thank you for this financing. It really sounds wonderful."

"Thanks, Greta, let's make a difference in some ladies' lives."

"I'll call the seller tomorrow and start negotiating." Greta said.

"Great, Hank can help with the negotiations. Give me the contact info of the seller and I'll put Hank in touch with him. Hank will get a lower price. Next time he is in town, you'll meet him."

"Perfect. And thanks, Lauren."

"I'm glad it's working out."

Chapter 33

Feeling pleased about finding the financing for Greta's project but apprehensive about the means used to get the funding, I walked into my office with mixed emotions. With Hank on the backburner, my heart was no longer vulnerable. In a weird way, it made me feel safer. What I didn't know was that my life was about to implode – *again.*

Just as I sat down at my desk my phone rang.

"Hello?"

"Lauren, what the hell?"

I froze. Hank really pissed. Is he just realizing my betrayal?

"What's wrong?" I asked, like I didn't know.

"That creepy Howard has a track record of unwanted sexual advances. I investigated him after I met him in your office. By the way you acted, I think he's come on to you. Why didn't you tell me? I'm insulted."

"Oh Hank, I don't know what to say. Yes, he came on to me once and has harassed another woman at the office. I didn't think it was appropriate to tell you."

"Why the hell not?"

"Because I didn't want to drag you into this ugliness."

"You've introduced me to plenty of malice; need I remind you about the blackmail?"

"No, I remember."

"Shit, Lauren, it is that type of behavior that allows predators to roam among us. This information needs to be known by everyone so they can protect themselves from that 6' 2" brown hair, pale-skinned monster. His small eyes have no life in them; he can't focus and he is twitchy. Not the type of employee, boss or friend you'd want around any female, much less you."

"I'm sorry Hank, you are right."

"Did you know he settled a rape case out of court? This is not the kind of person I want near you and I'm sure Paul doesn't want as his manager. What was the incident with you?"

"He told me to meet at Pappardelle's for a bank dinner. When I got there, he was the only person there. I wanted to leave, but he told me to stay to talk about business. He propositioned me at dinner. I said "no". I went to the bathroom and put my phone on record, but when I got back, he pretended nothing happened. He denied his advances. It turns out he has been sexually harassing one of the ladies in my group for six months and fired her the other day."

"This guy is a bad dude. Just reading his file is repulsing me. Please stay away from him. I'm calling Paul next."

Hank hung up.

***

"Hi Paul, Hank Tofar here."

"Hey Hank, saw you the other day and now a phone call, everything okay?"

"Not really, Paul. I have some information on Howard Glub that you need to know."

"Ut-oh, this doesn't sound good, should I be sitting down?"

"Absolutely."

"Okay, Hank let me have it. I wondered why you asked about Howard when we met."

"Sorry to be the one to bring you this news, but there is an extensive record on Howard's poor behavior toward women, including a rape case. How did you hire him?"

"He came recommended by a member of the board. I'm sure we ran a credit check on him, which came up clean. I assumed we checked his criminal history; maybe we got sloppy with him."

"All of the cases were settled out of court. I'll have a copy of the file sent to you."

"Thank you, I'll alert our HR and law departments about this situation. If we can legally fire him, I'm sure we will."

"I suspect you'll release Howard once you read these files. I'm sorry to bring you this news, but Howard is dangerous."

Hank hung up the phone, concerned if Lauren would be on Howard's radar once he was fired.

What if…

Chapter 34

A few days later, I scurried to an Al-Anon meeting and saw Greta looking happy.

"What's going on, Greta? You look so happy."

"I am. I'm close to completing the paperwork for the required licenses and permits for the project. I sent you the seller's contact info yesterday. Did you send it to Hank?"

"That's great news. No, I'll send the info to Hank tonight when I get home. There has been some distraction at work."

"Oh? What's that?"

"Hank found out that my boss is a sexual predator. Hank met the creep and didn't like him, so the creepiness was investigated and it turns out Howard is a rapist."

"Oh my God, that's horrible. Aren't you glad Hank found out?"

"Yes, but I'm sure Howard will be fired which puts me in the spotlight. Howard was heading to his boss's office when I left work."

"Please be careful."

"I will."

The meeting was about integrity. It was about doing the next right thing, even if it was difficult to do. My face reddened thinking about extorting the funds from Hank. Was that who'd I'd become? Yes. Using my perception that Hank robbed the bank and justifying that excuse to extort funds from Hank was a poor decision on my part. It's not who I wanted to be. I wanted to be a beacon of love and light for all humans, but I was clearly falling short. Theft and betrayal dulled my mind and my heart. Damn.

"Let's go for dinner," Greta whispered in my ear.

"Sure," I said sadly.

Dinner talk was about the Center for Caring and Hope. Greta had a design for the building and established relationships with government organizations that fund women's help centers.

I was happy for her and relieved the project is underway, but I was disappointed in myself. Was there another way to get the funds? Did I really have to attack Hank?

"I need to meet with Hank and review this project. The pace will be up to him, but I'm hoping to be part of the process," Greta said.

"No problem, Hank should be part of the negotiating process," I said.

"Yes, when can I meet Hank? We need to buy the building and get started on the renovations."

"I'll call him when I get home tonight. I haven't talk to him much in the past few days."

"Thank you. I can't believe how much you are doing for me and all the ladies I hope to help."

"It's helping me too, Greta. Helping other people gets me out of my self-centeredness and into a more generous spirit; I just wish I didn't use manipulation to get what we needed."

"Thanks again," said Greta.

We went to another Al-Anon meeting that night. I needed the help. Greta and I sat next to each other. Just as she was about to add another thought, the meeting started.

The topic was not resisting life, but embracing it – the good, bad and the ugly. Embrace the situations I don't want, really? I resisted the undesirable my entire life. It's going to take some work to embrace the good and the bad of life.

After the meeting Greta said, "Can we skip our late snack tonight? I must review all the paperwork tonight before I talk with Hank. I want to be able to answer all his questions without stammering or having to look up the numbers."

"Sure, no problem," I answered. "I'll set up the introduction tonight."

I had a few errands to run anyway and I was happy to get them done tonight, so I went to the library on Fifth Ave and 42nd St. It was beautiful with over a hundred cement steps leading up to a magnificent entrance lined with columns, marble and moldings. After doing some investigative work on a prospective company I was interested in obtaining as a client, I roamed up Fifth Ave and dropped off my watch to be fixed on 49th Street. It was subway time for me. Since it was later in the evening, the rush hour mobs were missing, but there were plenty of people using the subway.

It was dark when I exited the subway station by my home; but lots of neighbors were coming home from dinner or work. As I turned the corner from Lexington Avenue to walk up my quiet street, I felt a coldness creep up my neck. I turned around to see what was going on, but only saw dark shadows. I started walking faster.

The eerie feeling wouldn't go away. I was about to start running for home when a hand grabbed my shoulder. As he spun me around, I was face to face with Howard Glub. The beady, brown eyes were glaring into me. I felt the searing of hatred pierce my heart with his heavy breathing in my face. His breathe smelled like bourbon. I couldn't move. My brain screamed to kick him in the balls and run, but I was parallelized.

"You cunt," Howard seethed, "because of you I got fired today."

"Why do you think I had anything to do with that?"

"Because someone had me investigated and gave the reports to Paul."

"It wasn't me."

"If it wasn't you, then it was that bastard boyfriend of yours."

"I think you are jumping to conclusions, Howard," I said as calmly as I could muster.

He started pushing me down the basement steps to my neighbor's apartment. I pushed back.

"I'm fucking you tonight, bitch. You are going to regret crossing my path."

"What the hell Howard," I responded. Then I started screaming "Help" as loud as I could as many times as I could.

Howard smacked me across my mouth, my head hit the brownstone wall. I felt dizzy, disoriented and powerless.

Howard reached down to his zipper and produced his member. I wanted to vomit. He tried to pull down my pants, but the belt stopped him.

"Help me, please," I bellowed as loud as I could. Knowing I was close to the most violent defilement of my life, I kneed him in the groin and ran up the basement steps. I headed for home with Howard hot on my tail.

He grabbed my long brown hair and jerked my head down to the pavement. I fell back onto the pavement howling. My phone rang. Howard kicked me on the side and sneered, "You're busy; you'll have to miss that call."

Just as he started masturbating over me, my neighbor's door opened. A man whose name I didn't know, but had nodded to occasionally, came out with a hammer in his hand.

"What are you doing? I've called the police, I suggest you leave," he said.

"Another time, Lauren, you bitch. I'll get you again and you won't be as lucky." He kicked me again and then ran.

I passed out.

Waking up a few minutes later, police were standing around me with my neighbor telling them the story of my interaction with Howard.

"Oh, you woke up, do you know who did this to you?" the officer asked.

"Yes, his name is Howard Glub. He was my boss, worked at City, but was fired today, I gather."

"Okay, can you sit up?"

"Yes," I said as I gingerly sat up. My head, ribs and back ached.

"Can you tell us about the assault?" Officer O'Neill asked me.

"Yes, but give me a minute," I asked.

"Sure, no problem. Take all the time you need."

"Okay, I'm still a little fuzzy, but Howard followed me home from the subway, but I didn't realize it until he put his hand on my shoulder. He told me he was fired and was going to rape me. I'm not sure he used that word though. He pushed me down those steps over there and pulled out his penis. I kneed him and pushed him out of my way. As I ran up the stairs I started screaming again. Howard pulled my hair and knocked me onto the sidewalk. He was just about to masturbate over me when my neighbor came out and told him he called the police and he should leave."

"Your neighbor saved you tonight."

"Yes, I owe him a big debt of gratitude," I said, looking at my neighbor.

"Thank you for saving my life; he wanted to kill me," I said.

"Glad he left when he did," my neighbor responded.

"Are you up for coming to the police station? Then we have to get you to the hospital," O'Neill said.

"I don't think Howard had an orgasm, so there is nothing for the hospital to do."

"They have plenty to do. You might have a concussion, you need to be examined for bruises, cuts and any other damage. Believe me, you'll probably spend the night at the hospital."

"Oh," was all I could say.

"Ready to head to the police station?" the officer asked.

"Yes, but let me talk to my neighbor."

I said another heartfelt thank you to the man who rescued me. I found out his name was Sam. Even Sam was shaking after the incident. I thanked him for being so very brave and for coming out of his building. How could I repay his kindness? I didn't know – I owed him.

The police station matched my mood, gloomy. I answered more questions and went through the story three more times. Officer O'Neill was a gentleman. He took his time with me and was very concerned about me; I felt safe at the station. Could I feel safe on the streets of New York? Would Howard come after me again and, if not Howard, what about other sexual predators?

By the time I got to the hospital, I was exhausted. I was examined and asked to spend the night, just as the police promised. I was relieved to stay there. Hopefully, Howard Glub is in custody.

I feel asleep as soon as I laid on the bed. While I woke up thinking that Howard attacked me three separate times, I went back to sleep once I realized where I was.

I called Greta the next morning and told her what happened.

"Stay there, I'll be right down. I'm taking care of you today. This is my area of expertise, I got you."

"Thank you," was all I could say.

I laid my head on the pillow knowing I had to call Hank. What should I say? He'll probably feel responsible for Howard's action, which is not true. I was tired and bruised, I wanted to be left alone. I didn't want to go through the story one more time – but I had to tell Hank.

He picked up on the first ring.

"Hey, I called you last night. Everything okay?" Hank asked.

"No, not really. I was attacked on my way home."

"Attacked? What do you mean?"

It was time to tell him, I didn't want to, but it had to be done.

"Hank, this isn't your fault, but Howard tried to rape me last night. My neighbor heard my screaming and came out of his building with a hammer in his hand. He told Howard that he called the police and that Howard should leave."

"Howard wanted dominance and power over me and said he would rape me another time."

Hank was silent on the other end, but I could feel his mind churning with this new information.

"I'll be up there this afternoon. I'm so sorry, Lauren. I had no idea Howard was so vengeful and violent."

"I'm okay. Greta is coming to the hospital to take me home soon. I just heard Howard is in custody, which is comforting to know."

"He's going away for a long time," Hank said.

Chapter 35

Greta knew exactly how to handle me. She hugged me and whispered in my ear that she was sorry. She held my hand silently.

"Thanks for getting me, Gretz," I said blankly staring at the wall.

She squeezed my hand and said nothing.

I could hear the noise and see the movements of a hospital, but I didn't feel present; I was outside my body.

Greta said nothing. She was in no hurry. She was waiting for me to take the lead. Her gentleness was comforting.

Not interested in time, I sat there, perseverating on Howard's attack. I didn't want to think about him, but I couldn't get his hatred and venom out of my mind. *Another addict in my life, shit.*

Finally, I turned to Greta and said, "Let's go. I need to get away from my brain."

"It's Howard's doing, Lauren, it's not your fault. Don't beat yourself up. It will take time to heal."

"Thanks," was all I could say, not really believing time would help. She handled processing me out of the hospital.

We took a cab home and I saw the spot where the fight took place. It felt like it was still happening to me. My body cringed. Time heals all wounds, really? I have my doubts.

I offered Greta a drink when we got into my co-op.

"No thanks," she said.

I just wanted to go to bed and get under the covers; Greta sensed my thoughts.

"I'm going to leave," said Gretz. "You don't have to play host to me; I admire the courage you showed to fight Howard. It was a brave thing to do, plus it probably saved you from a worse attack. You are one tough lady, Lauren and I'm honored to be able to call you my friend."

"Thank you, Gretz. I'll call you tomorrow. Hank is coming in tonight. You should meet him so you can move forward on the safe house. Now, more than ever, we need a place to heal."

Chapter 36

The knock at my door startled me. With a door man in the lobby, how safe am I if someone can get up to my front door without being announced. I prayed it was Hank.

As I peeped out through the hole, I saw Hank with no smile on his face, only sadness.

"Hi honey," I said as I opened the door.

Hank stood there looking at me.

"I'm so sorry, Lauren. I called Paul and got Howard fired. I never dreamed that Howard would go after you. I have a potential lawyer lined up if you approve. We're going to make sure he doesn't get released from prison any time soon."

"Thank you, Hank, but I just want to sit tonight. I can't think of next steps right now."

"Of course, honey. Take your time. We'll work through this together. Just want to let you know. I made sure Howard isn't released on bail. He won't get out until a verdict is decided and hopefully that verdict is guilty. If he is guilty, he'll be convicted for ten years and serve around six years."

"Thanks for your help."

"I had to help. Lauren, I understand he threatened you, so we may get a longer sentence. We'll see."

"Great."

I wasn't in the mood for revenge or conversation, I just wanted to numb myself, but I couldn't. A pint of rocky road didn't offer what I needed, neither did alcohol or pills. There was no vice strong enough to evade this agony. I had to sit with the pain, accept the pain, walk through the fire burning in my heart…and head.

Hank ordered Greek food. I wasn't eating, Hank picked at his meal.

"I'll call Paul tomorrow and tell him I'm not coming into the office for a few days," I said.

"That's a good idea. When I talked with Paul about Howard; he thought I was joking. He now knows Howard's a monster. His first concern was you, of course, but the bank is at risk. Hiring a violent sexual predator can't be good for business. Who wants to do business with a bank like that?"

Hank continued, "I suspect Paul will be working closely with the public relations department for a quite a while."

"You know, a woman in my department got fired because she didn't succumb to Howard's advances. Her name is Brenda. I wonder if she could help with this case; we certainly could help her, validating Howard's sexual predator side," I said.

"Good idea, I'll let the lawyer know about her."

"Thanks, do you think the bank will rehire her?"

"Not sure," Hank said.

"You need to meet Gretz today or tomorrow. I'll ask her to come over."

I put down the untouched food, laid back on the couch and feel asleep.

Chapter 37

I woke up in my bed. Hank had moved me; I could hear him working on the phone along with his computer in the living room. As soon as I came into the room, Hank hung up, jumped up and walked over to me. He hugged me and said it took courage to fight Howard.

Guiding me to the couch, I said, "I'm calling Greta, you two need to meet to move forward with the women's project. There's a big need here."

"That's fine, but most importantly, I'm happy you are okay."

He slid his arm around my shoulders as we sat down.

"You know not all men are vicious and violent. I hope you haven't lost your faith and love of mankind."

"Of course not," I said resting my head on his shoulder. I wrapped my arms around his waist and snuggled into him for protection.

Closing my eyes, I tried to focus on the good of Hank, not Howard. He was a special man. I looked up and started kissing the soft luscious lips. He was responsive and pulled me in closer. I could feel my heart beating against his chest as he gently ran his fingers through my hair. It was a sweet, loving kiss, not hard or desperate, but long and gentle.

Hank cradled my upper body, wanting to protect me. I felt adoration and safe. He pulled away from my lips, wiped hair from my face, repeatedly kissed my nose, my cheek, the other cheek, my forehead and landed back on my lips with his tongue in my mouth. I drew in a breath through my nose and allowed the desires to shoot through my body.

What happened with Howard was not sex. It was dominance, power and humiliation. I wondered how someone could have an orgasm with such hate and violence present, but my thoughts returned to desiring Hank. Forget Howard. Snuggling into Hank and clearing my brain, I unbuttoned his pants.

"Whoa, there. Are you sure you want to do this? I'm happy kissing you," Hank said.

"I'm not sure, but maybe it's time to get back in the saddle, a test drive so to say," I responded.

"Okay, but you say any time you want to stop. I'll go as far as you want to ride me."

"Thanks, Hank."

We kissed for a long time. My lips tingling and a red chin from his late day stubble made my heart swell. Wetness was seeping out of me and a pleasure pulse emanating between my hips caused me to realize that I wanted Hank inside of me.

"Let's go to the bedroom," I said.

I wanted to be comfortable and not contorted on the couch.

"Yes," was all Hank said.

He took off his shirt and pants on his way to the bedroom, which was less than an eight-foot walk. Reaching for my hand, he walked me the rest of the way into the inner sanctum. I was happy he did not try to remove my clothes, but thought it was sweet he was in his underwear.

I laid on the bed fully clothed and asked, "Please lay on top of me."

He obliged and started kissing me again. This was turning into the longest make out session I had since eighth grade. I spread my legs for Hank to rest his hips between me. The hardness of his cock and kindness of his eyes made me feel safe. I started squeezing his ass as he kissed my entire face.

"I love you, honey. I can't bear the thought of anything happening to you. How about moving to Florida with me? I have a large condo, plenty of room for the two of us. I'll bet you could transfer to Florida with your bank."

It was too much, I couldn't make decisions.

"Hank, I just forced you into funding a project you didn't want to support. How can you want to be with me? I'm not ready to bail on the bank but thank you for the offer."

Besides, I had much work to do; but did I really or was I just inflating my self-importance?

"Okay, maybe it is too soon, but think about it, Lauren. The change might be a great thing for you. You don't even have to work if you don't want to."

"Hank, I can't talk about this right now. I'm confused, disoriented and scared." I felt lost.

I pushed him off me, sat up, rubbed my face and headed to the bathroom. More major things to think about, it was too much. I closed the door behind me and cried quietly.

Hank knew he had pushed too much and immediately knocked on the door.

"Lauren, I'm sorry, we don't have to decide right now. Honey, please come out."

Just then there was a knock on my front door. Fear welled up inside, I was parallelized.

"Are you expecting company?" Hank asked seriously.

"No," was all I said.

Who could it be?

Chapter 38

"There is a short blonde at the door. She doesn't look threatening, should I let her in?" Hank asked.

"Oh, that's Greta, the woman we are helping with the women's center," I yelled from the bathroom.

"Should I open the door?"

"Yes, please introduce yourself, I have to splash cold water on my face."

Greta burst into the apartment when Hank opened the door.

"You must be Hank. I've heard so many wonderful things about you. Hi, I'm Greta."

"Hi Greta," Hank said.

Before he could get another word in Greta went over to the table and started unpacking her documents.

"I can't thank you enough for your financial help to get this center opened. I'm so excited to move forward," she said.

"Happy to help."

"Since this is your project, you lead, but if you don't mind, I'd like to go over everything with you that I've done to date. Also, let's discuss my vision."

"Sure, go ahead," was all Hank could say. Her energy and enthusiasm were in stark contrast to my vibrations.

Greta, happy to meet Hank and discuss the project, didn't notice my late entrance. But Hank jumped up when I came into the room.

"Hey Gretz," I said.

"Lauren, how are you? Sorry to barge in here and take over the conversation."

"No, no worries, I've been resting, but would love to be distracted by your plans. I'm tired of the same, grim tune playing in my head."

"Sit here, Lauren, next to me," Hank said.

As I sat down and looked up, I saw Greta's enthusiasm and Hank's love. I realized how lucky I was. I had dear friends. I was safe and protected in my apartment and didn't feel vulnerable and frail.

"We need to finalize the purchase contract, the agreement with the architects and then the general contractor. I'm not sure about all the permits and licenses, Hank – do you know what's required?" Greta asked.

"Yes, like the back of my hand. Let's go over the negotiations for the purchase of the building. It's an abandoned building, correct?"

"Yes, the building has been empty for four years. I had an inspector review the building and he said it had good bones – whatever that means."

"That means the roof and walls are strong, but we'll have to check everything again. Do you know what you want in the interior?"

"I want a large room on the first floor, perhaps 50' X 35' with a stage for lectures and events. I'd also like several intake rooms where the women can talk privately with a social worker and I need a small office. On the second and third floor, I'd like a total of ten small apartments to house families."

"Okay, sounds reasonable. Let's meet with the seller tomorrow. What price are you discussing right now?"

"He wants $150,000, I was going to offer $125,000."

"Do you know what the taxes are?"

"No."

"Ok, they will change anyway since the building has been empty. We just want to make sure that no tax liability is transferred to us when we buy the building."

"Thanks, Hank," Greta said.

***

The next day Hank and Greta met with the seller. Hank was firm in his offer price of $50,000, shocking Greta. With her mouth open, Hank walked away from the negotiations and called to Greta as he was walking out of the door. She sheepishly followed.

"Don't worry," Hank said, "they want to unload this building. $50,000 is a bigger offer than they've seen for years."

"Are you sure, Hank? I do want the building."

"Yes, and they know that, but I'm the developer and they know I'm not emotionally vested. They'll call us back to negotiations."

Just as the elevator doors opened, the bank Vice President came around the corner, "Hey, wait a minute."

"Yes?" Hank asked, putting his hand on the elevator doors to hold them open for a moment.

"We will sell you the building for $75,000, it's in a good location," the VP said.

"No thanks," Hank replied and step into the elevator.

"Stop," the VP yelled.

The elevator closed.

Hank, smiling to himself, could hear the VP yelling in the hallway.

After a few stops at various floors, the elevator made it to ground level; when the door opened, it revealed a distressed VP.

"$50,000 it is," he said.

"Thank you," was all Hank said.

Next, the architect toured the building, listening to Greta's vision for the building.

"I'll have the plans for you within two weeks. Meanwhile, you need to have the water and electrical checked to make sure everything's working," the architect said at the end of the tour.

"Thanks," Greta said gratefully.

Chapter 39

I went back at work; it was a welcomed distraction. With no Howard there, work was enjoyable. My boss, Paul, came to my office just as I was settling in.

"Hi Lauren, you got a minute?" He asked.

"Sure," was all I said.

"I'm sorry for all this mess. I had no idea Howard was so vile. I was shocked when I heard he tried to rape you. Please accept my most heartfelt apology."

"No problem, Paul, you didn't know."

"Thank you. I hate to continue in this unpleasantness, but I have another topic to discuss with you. What happened with Brenda? Was there something going on relating to Howard's sexual appetite?"

"Yes," I said.

"I was afraid that was the case. We are going to talk to Brenda and ask her about her experiences with Howard. Depending on what she says, we may offer her a job. Do you know the extent of Howard's behavior on her?"

"I'm not in a position to say Paul. You should ask Brenda."

"Yes, I understand you don't want to speak for her, but I know you two chatted and Hank asked me about Howard, so I suspect you might have a story or two."

"I'll tell you what happened to me. Howard invited me to a bank dinner with my colleagues shortly after I started working here. When I got to the restaurant, he was the only person there. He insisted that I have dinner with him. I did. He came on to me and said he would make sure I got the best accounts that he received if I had sex with him. I went to the ladies' room and returned with my cell recorder on. He was trapped by that tactic earlier in his career, but I wasn't aware. When I returned, I couldn't get him to repeat any of the vile insinuations he proposed earlier."

"Oh, that's bad. He was using his position and power to get sex. I wonder what other ladies left because of his sexual advances."

"I don't know, Paul," I said.

He left my office with a concerned look on his face and slumped shoulders. I suspected he was concerned about the position Howard's actions created for the bank. It was a publicity nightmare, not to mention the legal ramifications.

I didn't want the court fight. I didn't want to face Howard again. I didn't want to relive any of attack. But I didn't want to run into Howard again either. What I really wanted was to close my eyes and have this nightmare magically go away. It didn't seem likely this drama would end soon.

Hank was staying at my apartment; he was working on his business and the women's center project while I was at work. The evenings were nice. Sometimes Greta came over and we discussed the project, sometimes it was just the two of us. It felt very comfortable and loving – until Hank asked again, "Have you given any thought to moving to Florida, Lauren?"

Did I want to move to Florida? Not particularly, I thought. I liked Manhattan, but it would be easy for Howard to find me in NYC. Probably not as easy in Florida, but did I want to move because of fear? No.

"Not sure I'm ready to move Hank. I like NYC and my career is doing well, thanks to you choosing to keep your assets with me, at least in the short term. Howard could probably find me in Florida, he knows we are a couple. It makes sense that he would find out where you live to track me down."

"He's not going to be a problem for quite some time."

"How's that, Hank?"

"He is going away for a long time. He attacked many women, tried to rape you and threatened your life. I don't think they let people out of prison with that track record."

It was a relief to hear, but since I did some research, I knew he'd get out in 10 to 15 years – almost certainly – not an encouraging fact.

Is Howard the type to take responsibility for his actions, own the consequences and change or does he harbor resentment and grow his anger until he feels validation for murder? Deep down, I knew the answer.

Chapter 40

One enjoyable thing about having Hank stay with me was the spontaneity in our love life. Tuesday nights, Saturday mornings or if we both ended up home early during the workweek, more fun. While sex was still enticing, I felt Hank wasn't completely present during sex.

Was he losing interest in me, feeling betrayed by my blackmail or gaining interest in Greta?

It was time for action. I needed to spice things up. I would play the aggressor – dress up and seduce Hank. Is it my imagination or my self-doubt that caused this insecurity in me?

I left work early Thursday, got flowers, wine and a canister of Reddi Wip on my way home. I put candles in the living room, a fur on the floor and two glasses of wine with an opened bottle next to them.

I texted Hank and asked him when he'd be home. He didn't know, he was going over issues at the building with the general contractor and Greta. When you are done, please come home alone, was all I texted.

In the shower I scrubbed and shaved everything and slowly rubbed oil on my wet body. I thought about masturbating before Hank arrived just to start the juices, but decided no. Putting on the trampiest outfit I could find, I was getting in the mood. Black thigh high stockings with a black lace garter belt started the look. A black thong added some mystery along with a pair of black, suede, very high heels. After adjusting myself into a black lace bra, I decided it was time to have a sip of red wine. As I sauntered into the living room I wondered how long until Hank arrived.

Should I move to Florida? I was insecure, still traumatized and nervous about living in Hank's world. The prospect of living with Hank had appeal, but I also wanted independence. And, what about finances?

I played with myself while I waited. In the middle of my second glass of wine, the keys jangled at the door and Hank walked in with Greta following close behind. Her mouth dropped when she saw me, followed by a smile. She walked over and whispered in my ear, "You look wonderful."

She kissed me on lips and said, "It's time for me to go, I'm sorry I arrived unexpectedly."

She looked longingly into my eyes and kissing me gently on my cheek that shot spears of desire down my back.

"What's happening?" I asked.

"I want you, Lauren." She breathed into my ear.

Awkwardly Hank said, "Hey ladies, what is going on here?"

"Nothing," Greta said quickly.

"Let's talk tomorrow, Lauren," she said turning away.

"Okay," was all I could muster.

These were my two dear friends, the wine was confusing me, but I didn't want Greta to leave under this awkward circumstance.

"I'm going to change into something else, both of you please help yourself to the wine and I'll be right back," I said as I blew out the candles.

"Oh God, I just saw your text, Lauren. I'm so sorry," Hank said.

"No worries," I responded.

Guess there will be no sex tonight, I thought, *disappointed.*

"How is the project coming?" I yelled from the bedroom, trying to establish some rapport.

"It's good," Greta responded. "Hank has been invaluable. We are completing the architectural designs, applying for permits, going over the zoning, electrical, plumbing, checking for any challenges and lining up the contractors. If all goes well, we'll break ground in two weeks."

Walking into the living room, fully clothed, I said as enthusiastically as I could, "That's great news."

Hank kissed me and said, "I'm sorry I didn't see your text. Guess I have to check my phone more frequently."

"No worries," I said as light heartedly as I could.

"I should go," Greta said.

"No, this is fine, let's sit down and have a glass of wine, I'll order Chinese and we can talk about the women's service center. Since the Howard episode, I feel more connected to this project and would like to understand the phases and processes a woman goes through once she is violated."

"The phases vary with each rape: the women differ, ages vary and there is no one 'act,'" Greta said.

"The perpetrator changes, the list of variables goes on and on. Everyone has a different physical, emotional, spiritual and behavioral response. Some ladies don't talk about it, some can't stop talking about it. Phobias develop, depression, disrupted sleeping and irregular eating habits happen frequently. Every victim faces fear. As far as recovery goes, the positive reaction of family, friends and work associates is vitally important."

"That's interesting. Do women have trouble making decisions?" I asked.

"Absolutely, I'll bet you are stretched at work, yes?"

"Yeah, I'm also forgetting to do things."

"You probably don't want to make any big decisions just now and go easy on yourself. It will take time to heal."

"How much time?" I asked.

"It varies for everyone. I can't say. I'm sorry," Greta responded.

"This is good information to know, thank you Greta," Hank chimed in. "Lauren, anything you need from me, I'm here. You were right not to decide to move to Florida now. When you are ready, if you are ready, we can have the conversation. I leave it up to you to discuss."

"You might live in Florida?" Greta asked disappointedly.

"No," was all I said, annoyed Hank brought it up in front of Greta.

The food arrived quickly, but I wasn't hungry. Hank and Greta dug in. Realizing I was a bit dazed from two glasses of wine, I started drinking water and listened to recordings of conversations with Howard playing in my head. Would he find me and kill me? Was he that crazy? Yes was the word that kept coming into my thoughts.

"Isn't that right, Lauren?" is what I heard when I looked up.

I smiled at Hank and said, "Oh sorry, I was daydreaming."

"You look tired, you okay?"

"A little distracted," was my response.

"Thanks for dinner," Greta said, "I'll see you tomorrow."

After she left, Hank sat next to me. He looked into my eyes and said, "I'm so sorry I didn't see your text. Do you still want to effectively communicate tonight?"

I looked into those beautiful blue eyes, but said, "Another evening."

Chapter 41

Despite his work and the women's center project, Hank found time to make sure Howard didn't see the light of day until the trial. After discussing the resumes of several criminal attorneys with me, we hired an expert rape attorney to keep Howard behind bars for a long time.

I understood the goal was to build a strong case against this serial sexual predator, so Howard is an old man when released. Hank's attorney built a serial offender case against my former boss; thereby needing more victims to come forward. The result is a longer trial, but hopefully longer jail time.

After a difficult workday, I unlocked the door to my apartment.

"Oh, I'm glad you are home honey," Hank said.

"Why?" I asked.

"I'm sorry to say this, but you need to go to council's office for prep work on your testimony tomorrow."

"Oh, when do I have to go to court?"

"I'm not sure, but it will be by the end of this week or next week, depending on the other victim's testimony."

"Okay, I'm feeling better and would like to get the testimony behind me anyway," I said.

"Glad to hear that, Lauren. This is an unbelievable ordeal you have to go through."

"Since I can't change this situation, I'm trying to accept this grim reality and do the next right thing every day. It's hard some days; I'm having trouble focusing."

"Oh, I think you've been focused just fine," Hank said with a big grin.

***

Everyone was solicitous at the lawyer's office.

"Hello Lauren," the receptionist said. "We've been expecting you. Please follow me."

She led me to a small conference room and asked, "Would like coffee or water? We have muffins as well. Are you hungry?"

"No thanks," I said.

Two minutes after she left, a big, burly, red-faced attorney walked into the room.

"Hi Lauren, I'm Chad Winchester."

"Hello Chad," I shook his hand.

"I'm here to make your testimony as damaging as possible to Howard. I also want to make this as painless for you. With the proper amount of prep, your responses will become more automatic and not so cutting at your soul. All that aside, I'm sorry you have to go through this, Lauren. Howard is a monster. We have found eleven other women that are willing to testify against him – that is just the ladies that are willing to testify. You know there are many more that are staying in their dark shadows."

"Okay," was all I could say.

Eleven women: Howard was out of control.

We started the process, "Tell me what happened that night, Lauren?"

Ugh, here it comes. We spent the whole day going through the descriptions and words for me to use about Howard, our interactions and the attack. We went through questions that his defense would ask me. Chad showed me how to look strong and show signs of vulnerability as well. If the defense got too nasty or aggressive; I was to take a break if needed. I was to be open and candid about the attack.

I was gaining emotional stability since the violence but talking about every detail of that night brought me fear. I felt exposed, but Chad was very encouraging. He complemented me on my bravery and feistiness to keep Howard at bay and the willingness to get on the stand and face Howard.

At moments I felt enraged and willing to stare Howard down, other times I got choked up.

"Lauren, it is lunch time. Do you want to go to Katz's deli?"

"Yes, I love the pastrami."

"Great, let's go. I like the Reuben sandwiches there." Chad said.

Walking into the smells at the deli took me back to sweet memories at the deli.

Chad and I ordered our lunch and sat down at one of the long tables.

"You are doing very well, Lauren," he said. "This is tough; most people can't be as exact and accurate as you are. With your honest and straightforward account of the attack, we'll be able to put Howard away for many years. In fact, I think we can get a restraining order that Howard will never be able to come within 100 yards of you since he threatened you."

"That is good news, Chad. Do you think we'll be able to put Howard in jail for longer than 10 years?"

"I hope so," was Chad's response.

By the end of the day, Chad announced that I would have to be in court tomorrow. I swallowed at the immediacy of my appearance. In some ways, I decided it was better to get this behind me quickly so I could move on with my life.

Would I ever be able to get this behind me?

Chapter 42

Wearing a black pantsuit with a white blouse, low heels and a scarf around my neck, I walked up the steps of the courthouse with Hank right behind me.

It was a long night with little sleep, but I was prepared for this meeting. I wanted to see Howard behind bars.

"You can do this, Lauren," Hank whispered in my ear.

I smiled at him and wondered how long I'd have to wait to get on the stand.

When I walked into the court, everyone turned to look at me. First, I looked down at the floor intimidated, but then searched for Chad. He was hard to miss, at 6' 6" topped by black wavy hair and that beet red face. He waved me over to his table and told me to give the answers we rehearsed yesterday. He put me in the first row behind his table.

Did I remember what we rehearsed? Not sure.

After the judge entered the court, I was called to the stand and sworn in.

"Do you swear to tell the whole truth and nothing but the truth so help you God?"

"Yes."

Chad approached the witness stand, "Lauren, thank you for being here today. I know this brings up difficult memories, but we need to understand what Howard Glub is capable of doing."

I waited for the question.

"Lauren, what happened the night that Howard allegedly attacked you?"

There it is, the question. I took a deep breath and recounted my fighting off Howard, his sexual misconduct and threats to kill me.

I lost track of time on the stand. I focused primarily on Chad and my answers, but occasionally, I caught a glimpse of Howard. Hatred was in his eyes, but he looked haggard, like a beaten man. I could only hope...

The defense council approached me. They were very solicitous, which surprised me. I expected aggressive, intimidating behavior, but thankfully, that tactic is politically incorrect these days.

Howard was caught red handed as my neighbor came out of his house with a hammer and told Howard to stop. The attorney was trying, very subtly, to put the blame on me. He asked why I stayed and had dinner with Howard after he propositioned me, why I didn't report Howard to management immediately and why I didn't go to the police.

As practiced, I explained that I tried to record Howard at dinner and that I was new at the firm. While, I was bringing in assets and building a good practice, I didn't know where the company landmines were and who I could trust. I discussed my interactions with Brenda and learned of Howard's behavior toward her. Brenda had already testified, so our stories collaborated Howard's craziness. I was coached on all these questions and provided answers that satisfied the jury.

We recessed for lunch, but I wasn't hungry. Chad huddled with me.

"You are doing a great job, Lauren. This is hard and you are exhibiting strength and perseverance. Where are you finding the courage?" Chad asked.

"I'm grateful to be alive, Chad. Plus, I don't want Howard to attack any other women. His violence has to stop…now."

I finished the cross examination successfully and according to Chad I didn't have to appear on the witness stand again, but he wanted me in court tomorrow in case any additional questions came up.

***

That night Hank brought me flowers and wine.

"I suspect you didn't eat much today honey; do you want Greek or sushi tonight?"

"Let's go with Greek, thanks Hank."

He opened a bottle of premier cru Chablis as my phone buzzed.

"Hello?"

"Hey Lauren, it's Gretz. You did a great job today. How are you feeling? You want some company?"

I looked at Hank and mouthed, "It's Gretz, okay if she comes over?"

"Sure, if that's what you want," he said.

"Come on over, Gretz, we're about to order Greek, that okay with you?"

"Sure, see you in 20 minutes, thanks Lauren. I wanted to see you after your testimony."

The doorbell rang before we finished our first glass of wine. After opening the door, she burst in and wrapped her arms around me. It felt loving and healing. I didn't let go, neither did Greta.

After an unknown length of time, Hank finally said, "Hey, shouldn't I be in this hug. I'm feeling left out."

As we parted, Greta grabbed my face and kissed me on the lips. "I'm so happy this part is behind you. You look more like your old self."

Looking into her beautiful brown eyes, I said, "Thanks, Gretz, your support is important to me."

"You have more than my support, Lauren. Anything, anything at all and I'll be here."

Feeling like a third wheel, Hank said, "Hey ladies, it's time for a toast to Lauren's success in the courthouse."

Hank poured Greta a glass and we toasted to freedom from fear.

Greta turned to me and said, "The women's center isn't open just yet, but I would like to have a social worker come over here to provide some council for you."

"No, thanks, I'm okay," I said.

"Lauren, you are doing great, but this is a very important time for you. You need someone to talk to who is a professional in this area."

"Why?"

"Because you don't want to bury fears, resentments, anger, self-pity, victimization or a myriad of other emotions. Now is the time to bring them to light, talk about them, feel the pain and be free of the chains that bind us to a negative past. Over time, your relationship with Hank could be adversely affected if you bury your feelings."

"Okay, let's set up a meeting."

"Great," was all Greta said.

Hank walked over to me and said, "Thank you honey. I don't want any ramifications from Howard to come between us."

"Okay, okay," I said holding up my glass, "A toast to two dear friends helping me."

"Very Al-Anon like for you to accept the help, Lauren." Greta grinned.

I smiled.

The buzzer rang, I went to the intercom just as the doorman said, "Your food order is here."

"Great, send them up."

I went to the kitchen, pulled out plates, silverware, napkins and another bottle of wine.

"Do you think we are celebrating prematurely?" I asked.

"No, Howard's going away; he got caught red handed. The jury seems to be clear on his assault of you and was shocked at some of the stories from the other witnesses. I think he is going away for a very long time."

Hank cleared his laptop off the table and we all sat down to grilled octopus, Greek salad, tabbouleh, yogurt, gyro meat and lots of pita bread.

"Yummy," were the only words uttered as Hank and Greta dove into dinner. I picked at the food.

With two glasses of wine in me, I relaxed.

After they finished chowing down, we went to the couch with refilled wine glasses and collapsed.

"I can't believe this phase is almost over, I wonder how many years' sentencing Howard will have to serve," I said.

"Lauren, put your feet on my lap," Greta said.

Surprised, I looked at her quizzically.

"You need to unwind and rubbing your feet will help take your mind off of today's events."

"Okay," I said as I lifted my feet out of the slippers and put them on her lap.

She grabbed my right foot in the middle with two hands and started twisting in different directions. Her hands were powerful, she rubbed her thumbs on the bottom of my arch, pinched and twisted my toes and rubbed between my toes.

"Do you have any oil?" she asked.

"Yes, in the nightstand by the bed," I said.

Greta smiled at me, knowing the oil was by the bed for fun reasons.

Hank chimed in, "May I rub the other foot?"

"Sure," was Greta's response.

I closed my eyes and longed for sex. The throbbing between my legs was getting louder, resulting in damp panties.

Greta was kneading my calf as well as the foot. It didn't take Hank long to notice. He rubbed my foot, but went all the way up the leg, which was immediately followed by Greta doing the same.

I was turned on but didn't know what to say or do.

I opened my eyes just as Hank was leaning over to kiss me. I smiled with his lips descending onto mine and his tongue thrusting into my dry mouth. His sweet wetness stimulated all my senses as I reached up to pull him close to me.

"We're forgetting our favorite social worker here," Hank said.

I looked toward Greta and she, too, leaned forward and kissed me. It was gentle, soft kisses all over my lips and cheeks. As she made her way down my neck, I looked at Hank, who had a wide grin on his face. He raised eyebrows as if to say, yes? I smiled at him; a look of relief came over him as he reached for my pants.

"Should we go to the bedroom?" I asked.

Everyone stood up at the same time. We left the wine glasses behind and walked into the other room, dropping clothes on the way.

Hank and Greta both approached me. Greta was kissing my mouth with Hank on his knees with his hands between my legs. He started rubbing my clit softly in a circular motion. He licked my thighs.

"Why don't you lay down, honey?" Hank said.

As I laid back, Greta moved down from my mouth to my nipples. She leisurely bit, sucked and licked them. Her hand rubbed my belly while Hank licked my button and upper thighs. My legs spread wider as every atom in my body spun out of control.

"Um, what about you two?" I asked.

"Just relax Lauren, you need some Marvin Gaye healing," Greta said.

I laughed and said, "Never enough sexual healing!"

"Sshh," Greta said. "This is for you."

I grabbed her face and pulled her to my mouth. Our lips met, tongues went into each other's mouth with passion and heat developing in my heart and groin.

"Oh, Lauren," Greta breathed.

I reached down to her juicy pussy, inserted my index finger and rubbed her clit with my thumb. Her back stiffened, she put her hands on her hips and swayed her hips back and forth with my fingers following her hips.

Hank looked up and put his hand on her breast and the other hand on my tit. His stiff shaft looking lonely. With my finger still in Greta, I got on my knees and licked his member. Hank groaned, leaned forward and licked Greta's face. She used her hand to coddle her other breast while Hank was kissing her, and I was groping her twat.

I raised my head and said, "Greta, while Hank kisses you, how about I eat you?"

Her smile said it all. She flopped on her back, spread her legs as I dove to her sensual center. Hank leaned over Greta's face with his hands on her breasts. I licked the luscious red velvet treat with my tongue going from the clit down to the vagina. After trying to get my tongue deeper in her hole I continued the wet trail to her taint. Greta lifted her hips for easy access. I was squeezing her ass and went back to the clit with my tongue. I used my mouth and nose to rub the clit, labia and opening to the vagina. She started to groan.

"Can I go inside of her?" Hank asked me.

"Yes."

After changing positions Hank adeptly inserted himself in Greta with his eyes almost rolling back in his head. He released an augh. While the hips met and separated Greta grabbed my pussy and said, "You must cum tonight, it is important to me. What is going to do it for you?"

"You."

That word made her explode. She crunched the sheets in her hands, lifted her hips off the bed and said "Fuck me, don't stop."

Hank obliged her driving his member deeper and faster into the wet haven.

Sweat was running down Hank's chest with Greta playing with her clit. Her feet flexed and every muscle tightened as she looked up, sent me a kiss and mouthed, "I'm cumming."

She and Hank thrusted seven more times as Hank said, "I have to pull out; I want to come after Lauren."

"I'll lick her, you kiss her," Greta said as she got on her knees and bent down to my V.

Hank wanted to protest but did as he was told.

Greta knew how to lick my cunt. She didn't start with the clit. She licked my inner thighs leisurely; she tickled the sensitive skin between my legs and then put two fingers in my vagina. Gently entering me, no hard pushing. She spread my lips with her other hand and nuzzled my nob of nerves. It felt different to have a woman between my legs. She didn't dive for the prize, but stimulated the whole area, focused on drawing blood to the region, not just the clit and the vagina.

With Hank licking my neck, I was on my way to cumming.

"Take your time," Greta said.

I did, she licked, massaged and tickled my legs, belly and hips. The bottom half of my body was throbbing, aching and longing for an explosion.

Greta looked up at me and said, "You are going to like this."

She put her mouth against my crack and swirled her tongue along the edges of my labia and clit. The world stopped existing, blackness descended and every cell in my body was exploding with pleasure.

When I came back to earth, Greta was lying next to me and Hank was on his knees masturbating over both of us. I smiled and drifted off into another world.

Chapter 43

Feeling particularly happy the next day, I walked into the courtroom with hope in my heart.

The prosecution and defense rested the case, gave closing arguments and the jury went into seclusion. *Now we wait.*

Greta and Hank were sitting next to me.

"Should we go to breakfast?" Greta asked. "This could take a few days."

Chad turned around and said, "Wait for an hour, there's always the chance it could be a quick verdict. If there is no response in an hour, go, enjoy breakfast, but keep your phones on."

With my stomach growling and the hour mark approaching, we were discussing where to have breakfast. The door opened with a court clerk announcing that a unanimous verdict had been reached. The blood drained from my head, sweat appeared on my upper lip and I looked at Greta terrified. This is the moment.

She reached over and said, "No worries. There's nothing to fear, Lauren. You are going to be safe."

I didn't feel safe with my heart pounding through my rib cage and wondering if Howard was going to go free.

Maybe the jury believed Howard, maybe the attack was a bad dream.

"All rise," said the clerk.

The verdict was passed to the judge, who read it with a poker face and passed it back to the jury to be read aloud.

"The jury finds the defendant, Howard Glub, guilty on all counts of sexual misconduct, rape, assault and threatening another person's life."

I closed my eyes, lost my balance, Hank grabbed me around the waist and pulled me into him.

The judge said, "We will recess until tomorrow when a sentence will be handed down."

I started crying, the verdict verifying my pain overwhelmed me. I looked up through the tears to see Howard blubbering. After a few moments, he turned to look at the people in the courtroom. Odd, I thought. It was as though he wanted to remember who was there so when revenge time came, he knew who to go after. His eyes landed on me, glaring, he gave me the finger.

Hank pulled me away from the moment and said, "You don't need to interact with him ever again."

I hoped he was right.

Greta said, "Let's go get breakfast. We need to talk about what this means for Lauren."

"Sure, good idea," Hank said.

With my heart still pounding, I was no longer hungry, but went along with the plan. Coffee didn't even sound appealing.

The diner around the corner from the courthouse was always crowded. Gray linoleum floors, black booths, bright overhead lighting and a faded orange bar for singles to receive counter service reminded me of many diners in Manhattan. Lights too bright, furniture worn and everyone hustling to get the clients served and out the door.

Hank and Greta were ravenous. Greta ordered a western omelet, rye toast, a bowl of fruit and coffee. Hank got a short stack, scrambled eggs, sausage, bacon, white toast and coffee. I got hot water with lemon.

"You okay, Lauren? We got good news today," Hank said.

"Yes, I'm feeling overwhelmed, but otherwise fine. Locking eyes with Howard in the courthouse reminded me of the attack; which is behind me, but it's uncomfortable all the same."

"Lauren, you are going to continue to feel a myriad of emotions relating to Howard and his behavior. Acknowledge the pain, bring the ugliness to the front of your mind, please don't bury it. You need to let the feelings, both good and bad, see the light of day. By looking at and discussing the challenges you face, they lose power."

"Makes sense, I'll do my best," I said. "No sense letting negativity fester inside of me."

"Okay, who's going to talk about the white elephant in the diner?" Greta asked.

"Why, whatever do you mean?" I smiled at her knowing full well we needed to talk about last night.

"Well, I for one, had a great time, but I do not want to come between you and Hank," Greta said.

"I am very grateful for last night, but I certainly can't keep up with you two," Hank smiled.

"Sounds like everyone wants this to be a one and done deal. Is that what I'm hearing?" I asked.

"Not really, I want you as my girlfriend and Gretz to be a business partner and friend, but I don't want things to get weird. Do you think we can all feel comfortable with each other if we have a threesome occasionally?" Hank said.

"I'd be happy with that arrangement," Greta said as she looked at me.

With all the senses on me, I didn't know what to say. I was still dazed from the courthouse.

I looked at them and said, "I can't think clearly; I had fun last night, though."

"Okay," Hank said, "let's say we had a nice time and we'll stay friends."

"Sounds good to me," Greta said.

"Me too," I responded.

I suspected last night wasn't the last time we'd be together, but...

Chapter 44

The sentencing was determined the next day. The jury didn't want to stay any longer than necessary, so they came up with the punishment quickly. I didn't want to be in court, but the attorney asked me to attend. I needed to know anyway, so Hank and I went to the courthouse. We met Greta there.

"All rise," the court clerk said.

"Has the jury determined the sentence?" The judge asked.

"We have, Your Honor."

After reading the slip of paper, the judge nodded her head. I could barely breathe.

The jury foreman read, "The jury sentences the defendant, Howard Glub, to ten years for rape and ten years for threatening to kill another human being. The terms are to be served serially."

Great, I thought twenty years sentencing, he would be in prison for 16 years, at least. I was hoping for life which, of course, was unrealistic.

I turned to Greta and Hank, but Howard caught my eyes. He was no longer beaten, he was looking at years in prison, but didn't appear to care. He mouthed, "I'm going to get you."

Greta saw Howard's message to me, spun toward me and blocked my view. Her cheeks were flushed, mine had no blood.

We stared at each other and needed a minute to compose ourselves.

"Listen, Lauren, this is going to be okay. Don't worry just yet. Jail changes men. We can get a restraining order against Howard, after he is released from jail."

Somehow, I doubted that line of reasoning would keep him away from me, but I faked a smile.

Greta continued, "I know this is disappointing. Since Howard is a sexual offender; but he has to register where he lives."

"Yes, but he can jump on a plane and go wherever he pleases," I said.

"Not necessarily, it depends on the terms of his parole."

"That's good news." But was it good news or were my friends placating me?

"I think we should go out to lunch and discuss this sentencing," Greta said. "We need to make a plan and follow up on our options."

"I'm in," Hank said.

The options didn't stop the fear.

***

Back at work, my hair on the back of my neck rose when I walked by Howard's empty office. I couldn't shake the gloominess. Paul came into my office and repeated his apologies. Was his apology because he didn't want the bank to be sued? I didn't know and wasn't sure I cared.

"You're doing a great job, Lauren. No one in the bank has grown their business as fast as you have, thank you. Hank's business helped, but you've brought in plenty of new customers without him. You are an important part of this team. I'm promoting you to Sr. Vice President and if things continue to go well over the next few months, I'd like you to consider taking Howard's job."

Bribery is how they'll dodge a lawsuit, hmm. I was sure the "if things go well" comment meant that if I didn't sue the bank.

The only good news was that Brenda was back. She confided in me that she wasn't sure she wanted her job back. Her production wasn't what the bank wanted and if she couldn't bring in a few accounts soon, she'd come under someone's microscope again.

"Why don't you approach Paul for new accounts since you can still sue the bank. Clearly, he doesn't want to be sued and is happy to use incentives to remain in the clear."

"Great idea, thanks," Brenda said.

Chapter 45

"I can't believe the Center of Care and Hope is opening next week," Greta said.

"It happened in record time. I've never had a project completed before the deadlines and with as few problems as this one presented," Hank responded. "What a lucky break, the stars aligned for this deal and it came under budget."

"Thank goodness," Greta said.

I smiled at my two-favorite people.

With the threat of Howard removed for at least 16 years, I was feeling better. Howard's office didn't hold the dread it once did. With any luck, bad behavior will extend his sentencing.

Greta had a marketing blitz and a public relations campaign underway. She also had government contracts where she was paid for providing counseling services and a safe place for women and their children to reside. Her next focus was to establish relationships with employers that would hire the ladies, either part or full time.

Hank and I grew in love and respect for each other. He was aware of my defects as the blackmail showed, but he forgave and loved me anyway. What a concept: to be accepted as I am. I had not experienced that type of devotion and love – ever.

"Hank, would you consider moving to Manhattan for a few years? I know the accommodations are smaller than your apartment in Florida, but it is cozy. Maybe you could rent a space for your office. What do you think?"

"Lauren, are you ready to commit to a full-time relationship? I'd have to spend time in Florida, but I could be here about 70% of the time. We could decorate one of the Sutton Place condos together and have it as our home. What do you think?"

I'd forgotten about the Sutton Place building. I hadn't seen the units, but they had to be elegant – Sutton Place was no slouch neighborhood. This wouldn't be my place or his place, it would be our place. What a lovely thought.

"Hank, that plan sounds wonderful."

"Really?"

"Yes, I love that idea. My commute will be a little longer, but well worth it, given we'll be living together."

"Lauren, you've made me the happiest man." He reached over and pulled me into him. His arms squeezed me tight. I felt a love that spread to everything in my life.

As we separated, I thought of life's challenges. Alcoholic husband, a robber for a boss, a rapist for a boss and most importantly, no real skills to handle the bumps of life. My world changed for the better only because of my willingness to accept responsibility for my actions and the guidance from a 12-step program. I stopped blaming, criticizing, and judging others – most of the time. I owned my mistakes. I took responsibility for my life and stopped wanting others to behave the way I wanted them to act. No one wants to be controlled anyway, especially me.

Feeling grateful that I found love in many areas of my life, tears sprang to my eyes. I had tools to help me handle life in a sane and mature way. I said a silent prayer of thanks to the universe. I know obstacles will present themselves, and frequently. Because I was desperate and life had me on my knees, I was willing to change. The bad was the good of life since it forced me to stop living unconsciously and become aware of my thoughts and actions. Most importantly and thankfully, I was willing to change.

Certainly, the bad is the good.

CPSIA information can be obtained
at www.ICGtesting.com
Printed in the USA
BVHW08205503052I
606340BV00006B/1625